HILLARY AVIS

Born in a Barn

A Clucks & Clues Cozy Mystery Book Four

Contents

Chapter 1

"One sec, I'm almost ready!" I swiped a broken sugar cookie from the cooling rack in the kitchen and used it to coax my house hen, Boots, into the bathroom. She followed me eagerly, pecking up every sweet crumb with little chirrups of delight.

After ensuring she had fresh water in her dish, I flipped open the lid of the laundry hamper, in case she decided to lay her daily egg while we were at the Honeytree Holidays kickoff event, then closed the bathroom door to keep her out of trouble while we were gone.

I rejoined my daughter, Andrea, by the front door, where she was waiting with her twins. My sweet grandbabies. They'd flown out yesterday from Chicago to visit for Christmas, and their presence made my cozy little farmstead feel complete. I had everything I wanted, all in one place.

Andrea leaned over to zip up John-William's red fleece coat, and I grimaced as the huge tray she balanced on one arm teetered dangerously toward the floor, sending the cookies on it sliding to one side. She'd painstakingly decorated the gingerbread snowmen this morning to donate to the bake sale fundraiser, and I hated to see them ruined.

"Let me get it!" I said. Andrea straightened and shot me a grateful smile as I kneeled in front of the kids and zipped their matching jackets. Two pairs of serious brown eyes stared back at me.

"It's not that cold, Nana," Izzy—short for Isabella-Sophia, a real mouthful of a name for a four-year-old—said. She swished her little bob, a cute cap of straight brown hair that she'd inherited from her dad. She and her brother might be used to much colder weather where they lived in the Midwest, but the temperature outside was still pretty cold for Honeytree, Oregon.

My farm had been blessed with the perfect dusting of snow for their visit—a rarity before Christmas. It had collected on the bare branches of the apple orchard and lay like a crystalline quilt on the roofs of my ancient barn, cute cottage, and extravagant chicken coop, and added the extra bit of seasonal magic.

"We're going to be late," Andrea said impatiently. She stepped aside so I could grab my coat from the hook behind her and pick up the fir-bough garland that lay on the table by the door. I hurriedly shrugged my coat onto one arm and opened the front door with the other. To my surprise, I very nearly ran into the fist of the man standing on my porch, whose hand was raised and poised to knock.

I recognized him immediately.

The dyed-brown coif of hair, held with more hairspray than should be legal. The round face with skin so unnaturally smooth that it made him look like a five-foot-ten-inch baby. The single, ice-blue eye that blinked at me like a judgmental owl.

My ex-husband, Peterson Davis. The last person on earth I wanted to see standing on my doormat. I'd played doormat to him for thirty years of marriage, and now he was ancient history—the kind that should stay buried. He had a large, leather rolling suitcase parked beside his burgundy driving loafers.

I would have thought he was a hallucination, some ghost of Christmas past sent to teach me a lesson, except that his other eye was swollen shut and seemed to be developing one heck of a black eye. There was no way I was imagining that.

I slammed the door and leaned my back against it, trying to decide what to do about the unwelcome visitor on the other side. Andrea eyed me warily, guilt creeping into her expression.

"Did you know he was coming?" I demanded.

She cringed, and the snowman cookies slid two inches to the right on their tray. "I maybe invited him?"

"Well, uninvite him."

She pursed her lips, which she'd tinted with a very festive cranberry gloss. "It'll be nice to have a family Christmas, won't it? I can't ping-pong the kids around the country every holiday, and it's been two years since the divorce. You should be over it by now."

"Eighteen months," I corrected. That wasn't nearly enough Peterson-free time to fully heal from our messy marriage. I needed at least three, four decades more.

"It's plenty of time for two adults to figure out how to be in the same room." Andrea nudged me aside and opened the door. Peterson flashed us a blinding-white smile, which made the darkening bruise under his left eye look even worse. "Daddy! I'd hug you but I worked too hard on these cookies to risk

3

dropping them."

"That's my Anda-panda. Always a perfectionist." Peterson chuckled, like it was totally normal for him to show up at my house after not speaking a word to me since the day I moved out of the Beverly Hills mansion we shared. He ruffled John-William's hair affectionately. John-William stared up at him, silent. At least it wasn't just me. I'd worried that J.W.—his name was as unwieldy as his sister's—didn't like me because he hadn't said a full sentence aloud to me in the last twenty-four hours since they arrived. But maybe he was just shy.

"What happened to your eye, Gamp?" Izzy squinted up at Peterson. "Did someone bonk you with their head?"

"Gamp just had a little accident. I'll be just fine, don't worry." Peterson pinched her cheek gently, earning himself a disgruntled pout.

Andrea leaned toward him to get a closer look at his eye. "Ouch, that looks terrible. You should get him an ice pack, Mom."

I pulled on the other arm of my coat and zipped it up, then scraped my hand along the porch rail, gathering a handful of snow. I squeezed it into a ball and handed it to him. "There you go."

"Thanks so much," he muttered sarcastically. He inspected the snow to ensure it was clean and then pressed it to his eye area. Over the kids' heads, he added, "When I stopped to gas up the Rolls, the redneck working at the pump scratched the paint. We had a few words."

"Must have been some seriously harsh words to mess your face up like that," I said. I had zero sympathy for Peterson's face or his car. Both of them could turn around and go back where they came from.

Andrea made a face at me and then turned back to her dad. "We were just heading out to the Honeytree Holidays thing so the kids can visit with Santa. Why don't you ride with Mom, and I'll follow you?"

"Your front seat is empty, too," I grumbled under my breath as I passed Andrea and headed for my car. I'd pulled my little Porsche convertible out of the barn earlier to gussy it up for the car show, and the red paint and chrome hubcaps made it shine like a Christmas ornament in the wintery landscape. I carefully laid the greenery garland in the back seat.

"Where should I put my suitcase?" Peterson yelled from the porch.

"Leave it there," I called back. Not like anyone was going to come up my long, gravel driveway to steal a suitcase full of Brooks Brothers khakis and pastel cashmere sweaters. I slammed the car door and started the engine, revving it to help the Porsche warm up faster.

Peterson looked back and forth between me and his suitcase before sliding up the handle and bumping it down the porch stairs. He locked it in the trunk of his gold Rolls Royce and then walked around my car to let himself into the passenger side, settling noisily into the leather seat. "Still driving this ancient thing, huh?"

I took a deep breath before I said something I regretted. The Porsche had been a fiftieth birthday present to myself, and I loved it more than life itself. Driving it was the one thing that'd kept me sane when my relationship with Peterson had gotten so clucked up. "It's only seven years old. That's hardly ancient."

Shifting the car into reverse, I pulled out and then crept down the driveway, killing time while I waited for Andrea to stow the cookies and kids and catch up.

"We'll have to get you a new one," Peterson said pleasantly. He flipped down the visor to check his eye in the mirror, pressing the puffy area gingerly with the tips of his pale, delicate surgeon's fingers, then flipped it back up.

I bristled at the word "we." *We* weren't going to do anything.

In my rearview mirror, I saw Andrea's rental car pull up behind me in the driveway, so I put my blinker on and turned onto the highway, picking up speed as I headed toward Honeytree.

Normally, the drive into town made me feel powerful and alive, as it calmed my nerves and reset my brain. But with Peterson sitting next to me, I felt like a wadded-up paper napkin. Used and wrinkled, fragile and easily discarded.

"You can't stay at the house," I said abruptly.

"Aw, Leona." He sighed. "I warned Andrea you'd be unhappy. Don't worry about it; I'll get a hotel."

A laugh escaped my lips before I could stifle it. "There aren't any hotels in Honeytree, sorry. We're not exactly a tourist destination."

"A town close by then."

I knew the quaint Victorian B&B in Duma was already full; guests often booked it years in advance. That only left one place to stay within thirty miles, a seedy motel next to the truck stop on the freeway. No way would Peterson stay there; he was more of the Four Seasons type. "I don't think the local accommodations will be up to your standards."

We hit the Curves, the winding section of the highway that led to the Honeytree city limits, and Peterson zipped up his leather bomber jacket to his chin, his teeth chattering as the chill breeze flowed over the windshield and whipped my blonde-and-silver ponytail into a cloud.

"I'll make do," he finally said. "Can you?"

I gripped the steering wheel so tightly that my knuckles went as white as the snow that dusted the canopy of the trees that lined the road. "Can I what?"

"Can you keep it together? For the twins, at least, so they don't see Gamp and Nana duking it out over the fruitcake?" In my peripheral vision, I could see him watching my face with his good eye, gauging my reaction.

I gave a curt nod. "I'll play nice for the visit with Santa. After that, you need to go."

Chapter 2

I pulled the Porsche around to the back of the library, motioning to Andrea to find a space in the lot while I eased the convertible onto the grass between a blue Pontiac GTO with a wreath on the front grille and a white Volkswagen bus that had blinking Christmas lights wound around the roof rack. A wooden sleigh nearly as large as the vehicle itself decorated the roof, and a glowing red nose was mounted between the headlights.

My best friend, Ruth Chapman, popped her head out of the passenger window. Honeytree's only hairdresser, she often experimented on her own locks. Today, I noticed she'd dyed the white strands in her dark curly hair a seasonal red and green. Silver bells dangled from her ears and made a cheerful jingling sound.

"What do you think?" She motioned to a deer antler that was zip-tied to the side mirror of the VW bus. "Pretty cute, huh? It was my idea."

I knew the bus belonged to Gary Edison, who owned the auto repair shop in Duma. Now that she and Gary were dating, Ruth had recruited him to organize the car show as part of the Honeytree Holidays, a weeklong celebration that the Chamber of Commerce organized every year.

It was all for a good cause. The car show, bake sale, and photos with Santa—along with other events during the week leading up to December twenty-fifth—raised funds for the Gifting Tree, a local tradition that provided Christmas gifts to the community's neediest children.

"Looks great!" I gave her a thumbs up and, ignoring Peterson, got out and scooped the green garland from the back seat. I draped it around the perimeter of the Porsche's rear seat, clicked on the star-shaped battery lights that I'd woven into the fir branches, and stood back to admire the effect.

Ruth squealed and clapped. "So pretty, Leona!"

"I agree. She's looking good," a voice rumbled behind me. I felt a pair of familiar, strong hands on my waist and turned my head just in time for a peck on the cheek from Eli Ramirez.

Once high school sweethearts, Eli and I reconnected when I moved back to town, but I was still getting used to the feeling of being one half of a couple. I'd figured I was done with committed relationships after my marriage went belly-up. But things with Eli were different than they'd been with Peterson.

Eli appreciated everything about me—even my sometimes-abrasive exterior—whereas my husband had always wanted to change me. He'd tried for years to mold me into the perfect, high-class housewife. This Cinderella never could quite squeeze her foot into that glass slipper, though.

Peterson stepped out of the car and cleared his throat, jogging my attention back to the present. "Introductions, please, Leona?"

Recognition dawned on Ruth's face. Despite our lifelong friendship, she'd never met my husband in person, but the video of him humiliating me on national television had gone viral, and Peterson, thanks to his regimen of spa treatments and plastic surgery "maintenance," still looked exactly the same as he had during the TV appearance. Well, except for the one eye that was puffed completely shut.

"I know who you are!" she exclaimed, pointing at him.

"Peterson, this is my friend Ruth Chapman. Ruth, Peterson Davis." I motioned awkwardly between them. He stuck out his hand and she shook it, grinning like a fool.

"You're the one who—"

"And this is Eli Ramirez," I interrupted before she could dredge up more of the bad memory. I stepped to the side so Peterson could get a better look at Eli. Peterson's good eye bugged out slightly as he took in Eli's full height, broad shoulders, and sheriff's uniform. Then he swallowed hard and extended his hand.

"Nice to meet you, Sheriff. I'm Leona's husband."

"Ex," I snapped. "Ex-husband."

"I knew what he meant." Eli shook Peterson's hand and clapped him on the arm like he was an old football buddy. "Welcome to Honeytree. I've got to make the rounds, but holler at me later and we can grab a beer or something."

Peterson gave a sickly nod—he was more of a white wine spritzer kind of guy—and, seemingly at a loss for words, watched Eli head off into the crowd of people who were gathered to admire the row of festive vehicles and vote on their favorite decorations.

"Where should I put the cookies, Mom?" Andrea asked, joining us. She lifted the tray she carried slightly to keep them out of reach of the kids. The twins tagged along beside her, each grasping a belt loop of her jeans so she could keep track of them in the parking lot even though her hands were full. One of those twin-mom tricks I'd never had to master.

"I'll take those!" Ruth said warmly, reaching her hands out for the tray. "It's good to see you again, Andrea! I can't believe how much J.W. and Izzy have grown since last year. Oh my word, did you make these? They look straight out of a Martha Stewart magazine."

"Mom baked, I decorated."

"Can I have one now?" Izzy begged.

"You know what, these are for the bake sale, but if you come on in, I will show you where Santa is." Ruth's eyes sparkled. "He might even have a candy cane for you. Do you like candy canes?"

Izzy bounced in her patent-leather Mary Janes. She let go of Andrea's belt loop and reached around the back of her mom's knees to poke her brother. "We love them, don't we?" J.W. nodded gravely in agreement.

"Well, then come on inside!" Ruth led us away from the car show and into the large community center attached to the back of the library. The expansive, well-lit room was teeming with holiday activity. Christmas carols played boisterously over speakers set into the ceiling, and as folks milled around the room, they hummed snatches of the familiar strains. On the stage at the far end of the room, a huge, green-and-gold throne and a sign reading "North Pole" were surrounded by fluffy, quilt-batting snow.

Though the throne's seat was currently empty, a line had formed to one side of the stage, and an elf in curled-toe boots and a plump Mrs. Claus were making their way down the row of families, handing out striped candy canes to keep the kids happy while they waited their turn to sit on Santa's lap. At the same time, they collected the ten-dollar photo fee from the parents.

11

Tables set up along the back wall, manned by members of the Friends of the Library, groaned under the weight of hundreds of delectable baked goods for sale, all donated by people in the community. Loaves of pumpkin bread rubbed shoulders with fruitcakes, pumpkin pies nestled up to Swiss rolls, and cookies of every stripe and type stretched out for what seemed like acres.

Ruth added Andrea's tray of snowmen to the array, then showed us past the cluster of craft vendors and the huge Gifting Tree in the center of the room. The fifteen-foot fir tree was decorated with miniature sweaters and stockings, and a long, striped scarf wound around the tree. It must have been hundreds of feet long. The wishes of local children fluttered on ribbons from the tree's branches, and the star on top nearly brushed the high ceiling. Underneath, toys still new in their packages—donations that hadn't yet been wrapped—clustered around the base of the tree.

As we joined the end of the Santa line, Izzy and J.W. crowded as close as they could to the family ahead of us. Andrea grabbed their hoods before they crashed into the people, but the kids in front of us, a pair of scrawny sisters with thin blonde pigtails, sensed their presence and turned around to gawk at us.

"There you go. Santa will be out in a just a minute. I should run and check the punch levels," Ruth chirped, waggling her fingers and then promptly abandoning me. Peterson and I both tried to avoid eye contact as he stood awkwardly beside me. I might have to tolerate him, but that didn't mean I had to talk to him.

"What's wrong with your eye, mister?" one of the little girls asked.

"He had an accident," Izzy supplied.

"Like a potty accident in his pants?" the little girl asked, and all four kids dissolved into giggles.

Peterson's cheeks flushed slightly, although his Botoxed forehead didn't even crease. "How much longer do we have to wait?" He leaned to see the extent of the line, as though measuring the length would tell him anything. Santa wasn't even on stage yet, so the length of the line didn't really matter. It hadn't even started moving.

"I'm sure it'll go quickly once they get going," Andrea said reassuringly. "Let's just relax and enjoy the family time. It's been so long since we were all together; I'm sure we have a ton of stuff to catch up on."

"Speaking of family, where's Steve?" He meant Steven Flint, Andrea's husband.

"Cardiology conference," Andrea said. "He's stuck there for a few more days. He'll fly out in time for Christmas, so you'll get to see him before you go."

My heartrate slowed until I could count each beat as I took in her meaning. Today was only December 20. That meant Peterson planned to stay in Honeytree at least five days. Probably six, since he wouldn't want to make the two-day drive back to Los Angeles on Christmas Day itself. Or longer?

I fanned myself, feeling faint. That was not good news. I could barely fake nice for an afternoon. How would I last a whole week?

"How many?" Mrs. Claus stood at my elbow, her pen poised above a small notepad that was printed at the top with the words "Nice List." The crop of gray curls under her velvet bonnet was authentic, but the round circles of blush on her cheeks and the padding that rounded out her waistline under the frilly holiday apron were not. When she wasn't playing

Santa's wife, Joan Packett was as narrow and pale as a parsnip.

"Three," Andrea said. "One of each kid and one of all of us together."

"How wonderful, a family portrait." Mrs. Claus beamed, jotting down the photo order. "That'll be thirty—"

Before she had the words out, Peterson whipped out his wallet. "Do you have change for a hundred?" he asked.

"Sure thing—or you could donate the change to the Gifting Tree," she added sweetly. "All donations go toward Christmas magic for Honeytree's most deserving children. Tax deductible. We got our nonprofit status this year."

"Perfect." Peterson produced his hundred-dollar bill with a flourish and handed it to her.

"Aw, Dad. That's so generous!" Andrea squeezed his arm and looked at him adoringly as Mrs. Claus moved on to the people who'd joined the line behind us. Peterson's eyes slid over to me, anticipating my reaction. I pretended I hadn't seen the whole exchange. It *was* generous, but Peterson was only generous when there were witnesses.

The elf, clad in a short green tunic and matching striped tights, arrived with candy canes for J.W. and Izzy. One of his rubber pointed ears slipped off when he bent to help them unwrap the end of their canes. I handed it back to him when he straightened, and he smiled crookedly as he reattached it, his dark blue eyes sparkling.

Those looked exactly like Ruth's eyes, which meant the elf had to be...

"Rusty!?" I gasped. A little over a year ago, Ruth's brother had left town to serve a short prison sentence for his part in a decades-old crime, but I hadn't heard he'd been released. Ruth must be ecstatic to have him home for the holidays.

He spread his arms wide. "Surprise! It's the elf, himself."

"It's great to see you! How're you doing?"

"Just trying to get my feet under me, find a job and stuff." Rusty plucked his short tunic. "As you can see, I'll take what I can get."

"Is this another boyfriend?" Peterson asked snidely, looking Rusty up and down from the tip of his green, pointed hat to the curled ends of his green boots. Andrea elbowed him, but frankly I was a little pleased that I wasn't the only one struggling to be nice.

"Just a friend. Some people have them." I knew better than anyone that Peterson struggled in that regard. He had employees. He had colleagues. He had associates at the country club and at various other organizations where he paid to be a member. But true friends? I'd been his only one. Maybe he should have thought of that before he divorced me is all I'm saying.

Peterson looked appropriately chagrined and, after a conciliatory handshake, Rusty moved down the line, whistling "Jingle Bells" as he passed candy canes to the next batch of kids.

"Tell Dad about your chicken farm," Andrea urged, sensing the tension between Peterson and me. "It's going really well, right?"

"Really well" was all relative. I was hitting my goals: selling eggs to local businesses, keeping my farmers market booth stocked in the warmer months, growing my flock to meet the growing demand. And my apple harvest and the resulting cider press had been fruitful to say the least. I was enjoying myself—that was my success—but I wasn't rolling in cash or anything. I wasn't successful by Peterson's yardstick, which measured profit rather than personal satisfaction. Besides, the guy didn't even have a goldfish—to say he was uninterested in animals would be an understatement.

"I don't think your dad cares about chickens."

Peterson made a face. "What're you talking about? I love chicken! Just talking about it is making me hungry."

I glared at him. "I raise them for eggs, not meat."

"See? We're catching up," Andrea said cheerily.

Now it was my turn to crane my neck to get a better look at Santa's throne. Still empty. "Where *is* that guy?"

Just then, Ruth reappeared with two glasses of punch. She handed them to Peterson and Andrea and then, with an apologetic smile, grabbed me by the elbow and tugged me out of line. "Can I borrow you for a minute?"

Relieved to avoid further awkward chit-chat, I nodded and followed her urgent strides to the front of the stage, where the photographer was standing next to his tripod, snapping his gum and scrolling through his phone while he waited for Santa to show up. "What is it?"

She kept her voice low. "You know Homer Wilds?"

I nodded. Homer was well-known around town, for reasons both good and bad. His business, the gas station here in Honeytree, sponsored many of the school sports teams, and his round belly and grizzled white beard were a fixture at home games. If your kid played football, basketball, or any other kind of ball while they were growing up, Homer Wilds was their biggest fan.

Unfortunately, he also hit the sauce a little too hard, and his fanaticism for sports was not improved by his liquor. He sometimes had heated words with the referees if he thought they made bad calls and would regularly get thrown out of school gymnasiums and soccer fields.

Ruth gulped a deep breath. "He's supposed to be Santa for us, but he hasn't shown, and he's not answering his phone!"

Mrs. Claus joined us in front of the stage in time to hear the end of Ruth's words. "He's probably passed out somewhere, as usual," she said matter-of-factly, fanning her notebook of photo orders. "We might as well start without him."

"Hi Joan. So sorry about all this. I'm going to try him one more time." Ruth fiddled with her phone and pressed it to her ear, catching her bottom lip in her teeth as she waited for him to pick up. After a few seconds, her face fell, and she hung up. "Straight to voicemail. I think his box is full. Probably full of my messages."

"We can't afford to refund all these photo fees," Joan declared, adjusting her cap. "I already paid the photographer and we're behind on Gifting Tree donations. Let's just have them take their pictures with Mrs. Claus."

"It's not the same," Ruth said glumly. "No offense, Joan. You look great in your costume. The kids just want Santa."

A Girl Scout carrying two paper plates of fudge squares paused by our small group. "Would you like to try some homemade fudge? I made it for a badge, so it's free."

Ruth and I dutifully took a square, but Joan waved the fudge away with a disgusted face. "Get that away from me!" she snapped. "You don't offer sugary trash to a diabetic!"

The poor little Girl Scout flushed. She looked like she was about to cry. Joan didn't need to be so rude to the poor kid. Ruth and I shared a surprised look as we sampled the fudge. It wasn't perfect—a little grainy—but it was a great attempt.

"It's very tasty," Ruth said kindly.

I nodded. "I like the sprinkle of salt on top."

A smile spread across the Girl Scout's face and she moved on to offer her wares to the families waiting for Santa. It was good timing; most of the kids had demolished their candy canes and were getting bored. They wiggled, crawled on the floor, clung to their parents' pant legs, and whined.

"What are we going to do?" Ruth moaned as she watched the whole line descend into chaos. The Girl Scout ran out of fudge about halfway through the line, and the complaints from the end of the line swelled.

Rusty jogged over to join us, his elf hat askew, the empty candy bucket hanging from his belt. "Don't take this the wrong way, but I think we should start. The people are already out the door."

Joan pinched the bridge of her nose. "Obviously. But the queen bee here says we can't until Old Sot Nick shows up."

Ruth's mane of curls seemed to expand around her head as her temper rose. She gestured to the long line that snaked all the way across the community center, the bells on her earrings jangling loudly. "They literally came to get pictures with Santa. How can they do that without a flip-flapping Santa?!"

Joan pursed her lips, the round circles of blush on her cheeks brightening. "Maybe you should have thought of that before you chose a boozing bozo like Homer Wilds to represent the spirit of Christmas without consulting the Gifting Tree Committee."

Ruth tossed up her hands. "*Excuse me* for choosing a guy who looks like Santa to play Santa!" Her voice carried across the room, and I noticed Eli's head turn toward our group where he stood by the bake sale table. Even the parents in line, who'd been too busy tending to their impatient children to pay attention earlier, looked over at us. In the middle of the crowd, Peterson and Andrea were staring, too. This whole exchange was getting out of hand.

I stepped between Ruth and Joan. "Let's take a minute, calm down, and come back with solutions instead of blame. We all want the same thing here, don't we?"

Ruth put her hands on her hips and glared past me at Joan, whose face was becoming more and more pinched. "What *I* want is some respect."

Joan sniffed. "I could say the same. I've been the chair of the Gifting Tree Committee for twenty-four years, and I've never seen Honeytree Holidays in more of a mess. We have felons playing elves, drunks playing saints, and hairdressers playing head honcho. One can only conclude—"

"Lady, you better not say it!" Rusty, who'd been silent until now, exploded. "My sister worked her a—

"Is there a problem over here?" Eli asked pleasantly, strolling over with his hands behind his back.

Rusty deflated and stepped back, staring at his turned-up toes. "No, Sheriff."

Joan opened her mouth, but I beat her to the punch before she could resume her slander of Ruth. "Homer's supposed to play Santa, but he hasn't turned up," I quickly explained.

Eli raised an eyebrow. "I'll swing by the gas station and check on him. Maybe he lost track of time." He gave my hand a quick squeeze. "I'll find you when I get back? I saw some mistletoe around here somewhere, and I want to see if it works."

I nodded, blushing, and with a flash of his most mischievous grin, Eli left in the direction of the parking lot.

Joan snorted and crossed her arms over her apron bib. "I guess I'll let the poor children know that they'll be waiting even longer. And Santa will probably be drunker than a skunk when he does show up. Lovely. Just lovely."

Ruth rubbed her forehead as Joan carried on, her posture defeated. Rusty, on the other hand, paced back and forth, his tension mounting as he listened to the lengthening diatribe. He looked like a volcano ready to erupt. I needed to do something before he totally lost it.

Joan gave Ruth a pointed look. "Even if the sheriff finds Homer in a ditch somewhere, he still has to haul him back here, stuff him into the Santa suit, and sober him up. I hope you have plenty of coffee and breath mints handy."

"Where *is* the Santa suit?" I asked Ruth. "Does Homer have it or is it here?"

"It's in the dressing room." Ruth sighed, motioning to a door next to the stage.

"Great, then all we need is a volunteer to put it on."

Ruth shook her head. "I wish it were that easy. When I rented the suit, I didn't get a beard, because—"

"Homer has a real beard," I finished. I scanned the room, holding my breath, looking for a decent substitute. At this point, it didn't even need to be a white beard. A gray one or even a salt-and-pepper one would do. But the only men in the crowd with beards were young, and a brown, black, or red beard was not going to cut it.

We were down a Santa.

Motherclucker.

Chapter 3

As I desperately searched the room for a second time for anything even slightly resembling Santa's beard, my eyes lit on the white quilt batting that decorated the photography backdrop. A slow smile spread across my face.

"Ruth, it's time to use your superpowers."

Ruth stared at me blankly. I grabbed a piece of the batting from the bottom of the North Pole sign and held it up. "You are going to transform this into a beard, and Rusty here is going to go slip into the Santa suit. The kids will never know the difference. All we need is a pair of scissors."

Ruth grinned at me and plucked the batting from my grasp. "Brilliant, Leona. I always carry shears in my purse. You'd be surprised how many haircuts I've given in the bleachers of a Little League game."

Joan looked skeptical, but Rusty immediately disappeared into the dressing room behind the stage, Ruth on his heels. They emerged mere minutes later. The kids in line quieted as soon as Rusty stepped out, their whines turning to whispers and gasps of delight.

Ruth had done a magnificent job with the quilt batting. She'd managed to shape the polyester strands to look like a natural beard. It wasn't the lush carpet of curls that fake Santa beards usually sported, but in a photograph, it'd look perfect. Rusty made a slim Santa, but once he was seated in the throne, the only sign that he'd once been an elf were his striped green-and-white stockings and his turned-up toes.

He noticed me looking at his feet and shrugged apologetically. "I wore sneakers today."

"Well, they call Santa the Jolly Old Elf. Maybe that's why." I grinned at him.

Joan looked him up and down appraisingly. "I guess that'll have to do. Let's get started," she said to the photographer, who'd been leaning against the back wall of the stage, listening to music on his earbuds. The photographer took his post and Joan led the first family in line to meet Rusty.

Ruth and I moved out of range of the camera, and she gave me a quick squeeze around the shoulders. "You saved my bacon back there."

"You're the one who saved the bacon. Nobody else could pull that off with just a pair of scissors," I said admiringly.

"Maybe this hairdresser *can* play head honcho, huh? Don't tell Joan I said that, though. I don't want to be on her naughty list again. I'm supposed to help wrap the Gifting Tree donations, so I'm stuck with her tomorrow, too."

I grimaced at the thought of a whole day with Joan. "I don't think I'd make it an hour."

"Come wrap with us," she begged. "Please? One, I could use the moral support. Two, we'll get it done faster, so I don't have to spend any second longer than necessary with her. And three, you'll be there to break up any fistfights between us." She giggled, but then her face fell. "Shoot, you can't. You have company to entertain."

I followed her gaze over to where Andrea, Peterson, and the

kids were shuffling forward as the line moved toward Santa. They were only a couple families from the front of the line now. Rusty and the photographer were doing their best to move things along while still giving every child the attention they deserved.

As I watched, Peterson glanced impatiently at his Rolex. His signature move: *I don't have time for this.* The familiar gesture made my skin crawl.

"You know what? I'll do it." The words flew out of my mouth. "I'll probably need a break from playing gracious hostess, anyway. You know I can only be nice for so long. And on that note, it's back to the salt mines—I mean the Santa line—for me."

Ruth giggled at my retreating back. I rejoined the line just as the twins reached the front. Andrea released J.W.'s hood so Joan could lead him over to Santa.

"Ho, ho, ho," Rusty laughed, patting his knee. J.W. ignored the invitation, instead standing on tiptoe to whisper in Santa's ear. Then he stood stiffly beside Rusty at a cautious distance until the photographer snapped his picture.

"Your turn!" Andrea let go of Izzy's hood and the little girl made a dash for Santa's lap. She crawled up on his knee and proceeded to regale him with a long list of Christmas requests as J.W. wandered back over to us.

Peterson nudged me. "Do you have any makeup in your bag?"

I snorted in disbelief. "I'm fine with how I look, thanks anyway. You can keep your opinions to yourself. I stopped caring what you think about my appearance a while back."

"Not for you—for me." The note of desperation in his voice made me actually look at him. His shiner was darkening up and the swelling was still getting worse, not better. I almost felt bad for him.

"All I have is Chapstick, sorry. But honestly, Peterson, I don't think slapping some concealer on your eye would improve it much, anyway."

"It's going to ruin the photo," he fretted. "Maybe I should just stay out of it."

I shrugged. "By all means, if you want to disappoint your daughter and grandchildren."

"Come on, Dad, it's a family photo!" Andrea said impatiently. "That means the whole family needs to be in it. When you look back on this, it'll just be a funny memory."

Joan came to gather the rest of us for the third photo, and I could sense Peterson's growing dread as we made our way over to the throne. He was so hung up on superficialities that he didn't realize this wasn't about him.

Out of the corner of my mouth, I murmured, "Just turn your head to the side. It'll cast a shadow so the bruise won't be as noticeable. Nobody will even care about us in the picture, anyway. They'll be too busy looking at the cute kids."

"Thanks," he said, blinking his good eye as moisture welled in it. "I just wanted it to be perfect."

As I took my place on the opposite side of Santa, as far away from him as possible but still within the camera's frame, I had to admit that, in his own way, Peterson Davis was trying. I actually felt a little bad for him now. He'd been punched in the face and he was doing his best to be cheerful and participate in a small-town celebration that, compared to a glamorous L.A. holiday, looked like something he'd prefer to scrape off the bottom of his shoe.

With that in mind, the rest of the afternoon was surprisingly bearable. We ambled around, checking out the decorated cars outside and Christmas crafts inside while the kids ran amuck with the rabble of other children who'd already had their Santa pictures taken. Maybe it was just the holiday magic at work, though, because the peace between Peterson and me only lasted until we got back to Lucky Cluck Farm.

When I pulled the Porsche in between my Suburban and his gold Rolls, he bolted out of the passenger seat and up onto the porch. He glanced at his watch as I got out of the car, tapping his foot impatiently. Irritation crawled up my back.

"Hurry," he urged as I made my way up the stairs. What was he late for, the bus? I hoped it was a bus out of town.

"I told you, you can't stay here. I'm sorry—I just don't have the space." I reached the porch and got out my phone as the crackle of gravel behind me told me that Andrea and the kids had arrived. "There are some nice hotels in Eugene. I'll call around and find one with a vacancy. It's an hour away, but it's not—"

"Just unlock the door," he pleaded, cutting me off. "I need a pit stop after all that punch."

He shifted his weight back and forth as he stood on the doormat. Was Peterson—excuse me, I meant to say *the prominent plastic surgeon, Dr. Peterson Davis*—doing the potty dance on my front porch?

Smirking, I reached around him to turn the doorknob, then pushed the door open. He just stood there staring at me, so I gestured to the open doorway. "Go straight on through. Bathroom's in the back."

"It wasn't locked?"

"Nope." I grinned at his dumbfounded expression. It might be hard to believe if you didn't grow up in a small town, but locking the door just wasn't necessary around here. Anyone

25

who let themselves in was a friend.

With a shake of his head, he dashed inside just as Andrea made it up the stairs with the kids, J.W. nodding in her arms and Izzy lagging behind. "He fell asleep in the car. I think they need a little nap. I hate to put them down because it means they're going to be up late, but if we don't"—she grimaced—"I fear for the dinner hour."

I nodded. "If they stay up, we'll watch a Christmas movie, maybe with some cocoa and cookies. It'll be fun."

"Just what they need, more sugar," Andrea said, rolling her eyes as she carried J.W.—and half-dragged Izzy—into the house and upstairs to the bedroom. If I weren't her mother, I wouldn't have been able to tell that she liked the idea, but I knew she was reassured by my suggestion. She'd inherited more than her blonde hair from me—she had a little bit of my prickly disposition, too.

The twins must have been exhausted, because Andrea returned mere seconds later, their red fleece jackets and two pairs of shoes dangling from her hands, while I was still hanging up my own coat. She stowed the items and then sank into one of the chairs around my vintage kitchen table.

"Want some tea while I get dinner started?" I asked, moving to put the kettle on the stove. But before Andrea could answer, a crash from the back of the cottage startled us both.

"Is that the kids?" she asked, rising to her feet. Another crash, the sound of something breaking, and a string of blue curse words.

"Not the kids," I croaked, as I tried to stifle a laugh. That was the sound of Peterson losing his mind in the bathroom, and I knew exactly why.

Boots.

Chapter 4

Peterson stormed into the kitchen. Now, in addition to his badly swollen eye, he also had a long scratch across his cheek that was oozing blood. Andrea stared at him from her seat, horrified.

"There is a *chicken* in your *bathroom*," he announced, like it was breaking news. "I tried, but I couldn't get it out. Did you know they have *claws?*"

"That's Boots. She's—well, she's a pet. She lives in the house. I should have warned you that she was in there." I'd honestly forgotten about her, with everything else going on. I ran a paper towel under some cold water and handed it to him, waiting while he dabbed the blood from his cheek. "Are you OK?"

"I was just sitting there, and—" he began, but Andrea held up her hand to stop him.

"Dad, TMI. We know what you were doing in the bathroom."

Peterson pulled out the chair opposite her and sat down. "As I was *saying,* I was just sitting there, minding my own business, and suddenly this *head* pops out of the hamper. The lid was wide open—you really should close it when you're not using it, Leona."

"I left it open on purpose. She likes to lay her eggs in there."

He looked at me like I was speaking Latin. "Anyway, I yelled

27

because I was surprised, and then the thing *flew* at my face. Did you know that chickens fly?"

"They're birds, Peterson. They have wings."

He rolled his eyes. "I was talking to Andrea. Did you know that? I thought they were, you know, like dodos. Ostriches. Flightless."

Andrea shrugged. "I never thought about it."

Peterson jabbed a finger at her meaningfully. "Well, watch out for them. They can fly, and they're vicious. I don't want J.W. and Izzy around them this week. It's too dangerous."

"Oh, come on," I scoffed. "The kids played with them last Christmas when they were only three. The chickens are harmless, as long as you don't let them peck you in the eye."

Peterson clapped his hand protectively over the swollen side of his face. "Well, keep them away from me. I can't spare another one."

"Why don't I call those hotels?" I said, keeping my voice syrupy-sweet. I stepped away from the table to get my phone before I socked him in the good eye.

"What? Why can't Dad stay here?" Andrea protested, rising to follow me.

"Where?" I asked, gesturing around my small cottage. I'd made up the guest room for Andrea and Steve and given up my attic bedroom for the twins. The only other sleeping space in the whole house—the vintage velvet sofa in the living room—was now *my* bed. And I wasn't about to share it.

"He can take the recliner."

The recliner, one of Boots's favored nighttime perches, was right next to the sofa. If Andrea thought I was going to sleep six inches from my ex-husband for an entire week, she was sorely mistaken. I didn't want to sleep in the same *state* as him, let alone the same room.

But Peterson was one step ahead of me. "It's fine. I'm not up for sharing a bathroom with that...that...*beast*."

"Da-aaad!" Andrea wailed. "You said you were going to try!"

"Anda-panda, some things can't be borne," he said grimly.

"But it's—"

"I'll be out on the porch, making some calls," I interrupted. I let myself out the front door and plopped into one of the Adirondack chairs, welcoming the chill that washed over my skin and cleared my head. The thin layer of snow, which had mostly melted away over the course of the day, still dampened the normal sounds of the farm. Even the pleasant soft clucking of the hens in the coop sounded softer and further away. I quickly searched for the most expensive hotels within fifty miles and made a call to the one at the top.

"So sorry—we're all booked up until after the new year," the nice young man who answered the phone told me. "Would you like me to add your name to the waitlist in case we have a cancellation?"

"Sure." I gave him my information and, with a sigh, called the next hotel on the list. Same story. By the time I got down to the seventh hotel—which I wasn't even sure would surpass the roadside motel in quality—I was ready to scream.

Andrea stuck her head out the door. "Did you find one?"

"No. I'm still trying."

"Who's that?" Andrea squinted past me, out toward the chicken coop on the other side of the driveway. I followed her gaze and saw Eli walking over from his blueberry farm next door, his arms loaded down with who-knows-what. He used his foot to unlatch the gate we'd installed between our properties during this past harvest season, once we got sick of climbing through the barbed wire to visit each other.

"Eli. You met him this morning, remember?"

Recognition dawned on her face. "Oh yeah. I didn't place him without his uniform on."

Eli raised his right hand and its contents—I could now see he was carrying a six-pack of beer bottles—in greeting as he neared where we were standing. He was freshly showered after his shift; I could tell by the damp curl in his hair. He wore a plaid flannel shirt and jeans, a puffy vest open on top in lieu of a jacket, looking every bit like George Clooney playing the Brawny paper towel guy. I was into it.

"I came to apologize," he said when he reached the porch. Now I was even more into it, though I wasn't quite sure what he was apologizing for. At my quizzical expression, he clarified, "For disappearing on you this afternoon. I said I'd come back, but it all took longer than I anticipated. But hey! I brought some mistletoe, so I can at least fulfill that part of my promise." He smiled crookedly and held up the bunch of greenery in his other hand—as high as he could without dropping the paper-wrapped package he had clamped under his arm.

"Did you find Homer?" I asked.

He nodded slowly. "I did. At the gas station. He was—" He broke off and glanced at Andrea and then back to me, seemingly unsure whether he could speak freely in front of her. I gave him a nod and he finished his sentence. "Dead."

Andrea's mouth dropped open.

"What are you guys up to?" Eli asked cheerily, moving toward the door. "Can you get the door? I should probably put the beer in the fridge. I didn't know what kind Peterson drinks, so I brought a holiday ale *and* a stout."

"Back up," Andrea said. "Did you just say 'dead'?"

"Unfortunately." Eli's expression turned serious, but he didn't elaborate. I pushed open the door for him, and he headed for the kitchen.

"That's the reality of being a law enforcement officer," I explained to Andrea as we followed him in. "He's there for all the worst stuff."

Peterson scraped back his chair and stood up abruptly when he saw Eli enter, his face paling and setting his bruise and new scratch in high relief. "What're you doing here?"

"Brought you a steak for that eye, Buddy," Eli said, stepping around him and sliding the beer into the fridge next to a stack of three egg cartons. "I noticed that shiner—and extras for dinner, if you don't already have something in the oven." This last part was to me. He handed me the paper-wrapped package.

"Nope. We were busy trying to find Peterson a hotel. No luck, though." I turned to the counter and unwrapped the steaks; they were beautiful—too nice to slap on someone's black eye, I thought, but Eli reached around me and grabbed the smallest one. He held it out to Peterson, who made a face.

"I am *not* putting raw meat on my eye. That can't be sanitary."

"Suit yourself." Eli shrugged and dropped it back on the paper. He nudged me playfully and held up the huge handful of mistletoe. It looked like he'd just grabbed a whole bush. The recent windstorms had blown many mistletoe plants out of the tops of oak trees in the area. It wasn't hard to find a big bunch laying in a field or on the side of the road. "Where should I hang this? A sprig in every doorway?"

I grinned at his eager expression, but there was no way I could handle that much mistletoe, not when my ex-husband was hanging around like flies on manure. "Let's keep the mistletoe to one zone so we don't get ourselves into too much trouble."

"A single mistletoe zone, you got it." Eli dragged the stepstool out of the pantry and positioned it in the center of the doorway between the kitchen and the entryway.

Andrea let out a screech. "Why isn't anyone talking about the dead guy at the gas station? What happened to him?"

Peterson made a strangled sound, and his legs gave out. Eli reached out and caught his elbow just in time to keep him from falling to the floor.

"You OK, Buddy?" Eli asked as he helped Peterson back to his seat at the table.

Peterson shook his head *no*. Andrea, frozen where she stood, made silent movements with her mouth, like she was saying a prayer or rehearsing her lines for a play.

Finally, she asked, "What happened to him?"

"Not sure. He was beat up pretty good, and the cash drawer only had a couple bucks in it, so we're thinking a robbery gone wrong, maybe? We'll have a better handle on cause of death when the autopsy comes back." Eli hung a bunch of the mistletoe from the doorway and then dipped into the pantry to put the stepstool away. He returned with a bag of russets and held them up. "What do you think, baked or mashed?"

"Mashed." I pulled out my favorite cast-iron skillet and set it on the stove. Eli took the bag of potatoes over to the sink and rinsed the mistletoe dust off his hands before he started peeling them. I got out the fixings for a green salad. We often cooked dinner together, alternating between our houses, and we'd found a pleasant rhythm in the kitchen.

"Dad?" Andrea pulled a chair close to Peterson and peered at his face. He was so gray that his round face, with its deepening bruise, looked like a full moon. "What happened after he hit you? Did you hit him back?"

Eli and I both froze.

"Wait. Which gas station did you stop at this morning?" I'd assumed the one near I5. It was the closest one to my farm, the one he'd pass on the way here.

"Wilds Gas and Go," Peterson mumbled, staring at the worn surface of my kitchen table, his long, pale fingers laced together.

"You went all the way to Remembrance for gas? That's so far out of the way. Why didn't you stop at—"

"I took the wrong exit, OK?" Peterson's voice took on a hard edge. "Get off my case, Leona."

"She's not the one on your case now," Eli growled. He plopped down opposite Peterson and stared across the table at him. "I am."

Chapter 5

"Let me get this story straight. Homer Wilds gave you that black eye?" Eli studied Peterson's face across the table.

Peterson nodded, his expression sickly. I handed him the salad bowl I'd intended to fill with greens in case he upchucked. He gripped it close to his body like it was a teddy bear. "I stopped to get gas. He was falling-down drunk, as far as I could tell. He accidentally banged the Rolls with the gas nozzle, so I got out to check the damage. The paint had a huge ding. We had some…words," he finished lamely.

"You lost your temper." Eli made it a statement, not a question. "Understandable."

I frowned. "It shouldn't have been a big deal, Peterson. You have insurance."

"I don't want to drive around here in a scratched-up car!" Peterson's good eye blazed. "What'll people think?"

I rolled my eyes at him. "So you punched a guy? That's a surefire way to improve people's opinion of you."

"Judging by what I saw, it was a lot more than one punch," Eli said quietly.

Andrea stiffened. "How bad?"

"Bad."

"He was stumbling all over." The color was returning to Peterson's cheeks now that his shock had worn off. "He kept crashing into stuff. Half of it, he did to himself."

Eli raised an eyebrow. "And the other half?"

"He was alive when I left. That's all I know." Peterson set the salad bowl on the table and crossed his arms defensively.

Andrea reached out to rub Peterson's back like she was comforting one of the twins. "It's OK, Dad. This is all going to be fine." She raised her head to look directly at Eli. "My dad didn't kill anyone—look at his hands."

Our eyes all went to Peterson's hands, which were clamped tightly around his thin upper arms. Pale, smooth, and perfect. No bruises or scrapes.

Eli visibly relaxed. "Tomorrow, I'd like you to walk me through your encounter with Homer Wilds, if you don't mind. It might help move the investigation in the right direction while we're waiting for the autopsy report to come back."

Peterson gave a terse nod. "Of course."

"I can pick you up here in the morning," Eli added. "I'd prefer if you didn't take your car anywhere." He didn't need to say why. We all understood his meaning. *In case it's evidence.*

"You can pick him up at his hotel," I corrected, turning back to my salad preparations. "If he can find one. Otherwise he might be sleeping in that car."

"Do you realize what you're saying, Mom?" Andrea asked, indignance creeping into her voice. "Are you really still saying there's *no room at the inn* for the father of your children?"

"Child," I said, stabbing the tomato a little harder than I needed to. "We have one child together."

"It's Christmas," she reminded me.

"Fine. He can stay in the barn, like Jesus." It was the perfect

35

solution, actually. Before the harvest this year, I'd refurbished the loft into rustic accommodations for my apple-picking crew. The previous owner, Ruth's grandfather, had used the space for his farm help, too. I'd improved his bare-bones set-up with comfortable beds, wool blankets, and a woodstove. It wasn't the Four Seasons, but it was better than the motel, that was for sure.

"He's not an animal! Anyway, you don't even make your chicken sleep in the barn!" Andrea yelped.

"It's nice!" I protested, turning back around to face the group. "There's even a private outhouse."

Peterson's upper lip trembled, sweat beading on his forehead. "It's fine, Andrea. If Leona doesn't want me here, I don't want to be here. I'm going to head home—this family Christmas thing was all a bad idea."

"I'm afraid you can't do that," Eli said, drawing the words out as he watched Peterson, his eyes narrowed. "I need you to stick around town until the autopsy comes back."

"Like Andrea said, I didn't kill him!" Peterson insisted, holding out his hands and flexing his fingers, presumably so Eli could view their undamaged lengths again.

Eli nodded. "I believe you. I do. But you may be the last person to see him alive. That makes you an important witness. I just want to make sure everything in the case is plumb before you leave town. Shouldn't be more than a few days. And in the meantime, I'm afraid I'll need your car keys."

Peterson pinched the bridge of his nose, wincing as his fingers grazed his swollen eye. Then he pulled his keys out of his pocket and handed them to Eli. "Fine."

"Leona will find some space for you—right?" Eli asked me. "The couch, maybe?"

"I'm already sleeping on the couch, and trust me, there's only room for one." I finished cutting the tomato into wedges and turned my attention to the cucumber.

"Let him have it. Come stay at my house."

I brought the knife down hard on the cucumber, splitting it in two. I pointed the knife at Eli, whose eyes twinkled at me. "I am *not* giving up my house to him. I worked hard for this farm, and he can't just waltz in here and take over my life. I divorced him for a reason, and it was because I spent thirty years giving up everything I wanted for his wants and needs."

"Was it really that bad?" Peterson asked. "Was our life together really that—"

"He can have the upstairs room," Andrea interrupted, her voice exhausted. "I'll move the kids down with me."

"No! No, no, no," I said, mutilating the poor cucumber even further by punctuating my words with slashes of the knife. The upstairs room was *my* bedroom. No way was Peterson sleeping in my bed. I didn't even let Eli stay the night, and I actually liked him.

"Whoa, Nellie." Eli reached around me and pried the knife handle out of my grip. "You're swinging a little wild there, partner. Peterson can stay with me. I've got two extra bedrooms and he can have his pick."

I felt the tension drain out of my shoulders at his suggestion. "Really? You'd do that? He's a terrible guest. He doesn't even know how to load a dishwasher."

"Of course." Eli gave me a reassuring smile. "Couple of guys, couple of brewskis, couple of ballgames? We'll have a great time."

"Maybe I should come stay with you, too," Andrea muttered. I shot her a look, and she rolled her eyes at me. "Just kidding."

"Do you mind if we head over now?" Peterson rose shakily from the table. "I'd like to lie down."

Andrea frowned. "Before dinner?"

"I don't have much of an appetite, I'm afraid."

"Understandable," Eli said. He handed me the kitchen knife back and headed toward the door. "Do you have some luggage you want to bring over?"

"Yeah, it's in the trunk," Peterson said, following him toward the front door.

"What about the steak?" I stood in the middle of the kitchen and gestured with the knife at the pile of half-peeled vegetables in the sink. "What about the potatoes?"

"Cook 'em. We can have the leftovers for breakfast," Eli said over his shoulder. The door banged shut behind them and I heard the soft beep-beep of the Rolls unlocking in the driveway outside.

Andrea went to the sink and began furiously peeling the remaining potatoes. "At least your *boyfriend* is nice to your family," she mumbled into the pile of peelings. "If you had your way, Dad would be in handcuffs right now."

"He's not my family," I said firmly, scooping my mauled cucumber pieces into the salad bowl along with the tomato wedges. "So I don't have to be nice to him anymore. Especially not when he barges into my life just to ruin my Christmas."

"Is that why you think he's here?" Andrea put down her peeler and turned her head to stare at me. "*Seriously*? He's here because I asked him to come, and you know why? Because every week, he's crying on the phone to me about how stupid he was to let you go. How he ruined everything up by taking you for granted. He knows he screwed up."

"I gather his girlfriend broke up with him?" As soon as we'd separated, before I'd even moved out of the house, Peterson had taken up with a model even younger than Andrea and let her move into the pool house. I found it hard to believe that his change of heart didn't have something to do with *her* change of heart.

"Well, there's that. But actually, he broke up with her, not the other way around, because she kept asking him for money. Plus, they had nothing in common."

"Surprise, surprise," I muttered to the salad.

"He wants to make amends. Give him a chance to show you how he's changed, Mom." Andrea bit her lip, her perfectly arched brows drawn together anxiously. "Please, can you stop being so harsh and just try to achieve some basic level of family harmony? For me and the kids?"

Well, when she put it that way, I couldn't refuse my own daughter. I took a deep breath and gave a single grudging nod. "I'll try to be nicer. For you and the kids."

Chapter 6

December 21

The twins were still in their pajamas when Peterson and Eli arrived the next morning. I'd already dressed in my comfiest pair of jeans and my pink-and-purple "World's Best Nana" T-shirt. I hoped the shirt's slogan would remind me of my promise to Andrea: I was going to be nice to Peterson—or at least *try*—for Andrea and J.W. and Izzy's sake.

"Have a seat; breakfast is almost ready," I said over my shoulder as I deftly flipped the potato pancakes. I turned up the radio so I could hear my favorite Christmas carol, *Twelve Days of Christmas*, over the sizzle of the griddle. I couldn't help being fond of it, given that it was one of the few songs in existence that featured chickens.

"Hi Gamp. Hi Other Guy," Izzy said, her face already smudged from the blueberry smoothie I'd made to tide the kids over while they waited for the real breakfast to cook. J.W. just blinked and slurped his straw.

"That's Eli, honey." Andrea reached over with a napkin and wiped Izzy's chin. "You guys have a good night?"

"We sure did. Watched some b-ball, ate TV dinners. Felt like

we were in our twenties again. Breakfast smells great, Leona."
Eli cleared his throat. "Anything I can help with?"

"Sure, you can grab the plates and set the table."

"I'll do it," Peterson said, stepping around him. He began
opening cupboards left and right, looking for the plates. The
swelling in his black eye was even worse than yesterday, and
the bruising had spread down his cheekbone like chocolate
sauce dripping down a sundae. It looked truly awful.

"They're right there, Eagle Eye." Eli nodded to the stack on
the counter, chuckling. "I'll get the forks."

The joint table-setting endeavor seemed a little competitive.
They both raced to finish their task first. Peterson slung his last
plate like a Frisbee, barely edging out Eli, who groaned with
disappointment as he placed the final fork.

Boys.

"You're lucky that plate didn't crack," I said to Peterson as I
hefted the big skillet of potatoes and eggs to the table and put
it down next to the leftover steak. Andrea shot me a warning
look, but I *was* being nice.

The rest of breakfast was amicable. Andrea kept the conversation going as she described their daily life in Chicago and asked
nice, neutral questions about life in Oregon. It wasn't until Izzy
recounted the Christmas list she'd told Santa in excruciating
detail that I remembered the serious reason for our gathering.
The "real" Santa was dead, and Peterson was the last one to see
him alive.

My appetite vanished even though my plate was still half full.
I pushed back my chair and gathered some empty dishes to
rinse in the sink. The window over it had a perfect view of
my coop and run, which was full of a couple hundred laying
hens and my glorious rooster, Alarm Clock. I'd decorated it

this year with a string of colorful lights around the eaves, but they looked less cheerful in the daylight.

Up the rise behind the coop, Eli's white farmhouse was visible. His large blueberry orchard stretched in rows between the fence and his driveway on the other side of the field. The blueberry bushes had turned a lovely purple-red shade during the fall, but now the leaves had all fallen, leaving the branches starkly bare. Yesterday's snow had melted away, leaving everything slightly gray and sodden. The effect was heightened by the heavy, dark clouds that hung over everything.

I shivered as I put the plates in the dishwasher. "We should get going, in case it decides to rain."

Eli scraped back his chair. "You don't have to come. I'll take good care of Pete, scout's honor." He held his fingers up in a mock salute.

"She can come if she wants," Peterson said irritably. My eyes flicked to him, surprised that he'd come to my defense. Andrea raised her eyebrows at me, as if to say *See? He really has changed.*

"I need to drop an order at the diner," I explained. The Greasy Spoon had an extensive breakfast menu, and as a result, was one of my most reliable egg customers. It just happened to be located right across the street from the gas station. "I'll meet up with you guys once I'm done and drive Peterson back, so you don't have to make an extra trip."

"I'll finish the dishes, Mom," Andrea volunteered. "The kids love helping with anything that involves bubbles."

Grateful, I dried my hands on the dish towel and went out to wrangle some eggs out of the fridge on the back porch. Eli and Peterson were gone by the time I got the specially fitted egg coolers in the Suburban loaded up. I had to drive differently to protect the small fortune of eggs in the back of my vehicle.

My Porsche wouldn't recognize the delicate handling I gave my Suburban when it was loaded up like this.

As I pulled in behind the diner to deliver the eggs, I noticed caution tape encircling the gas station building and pump across the street. A "closed" sign hung in the window of the small attached convenience store. Eli's SUV was parked in the lot nearby, but no other law enforcement officers were on the scene. That buoyed my hopes—nobody at the sheriff's office really thought Homer had been murdered. If they did, they'd have been swarming the place.

Homer had been falling-down drunk when Peterson stopped to get gas, he'd said. Alcohol was the more likely culprit of any harm that had come to Homer. He probably just passed out and hit his head on the hard, concrete floor. Maybe all the bumps and bruises he'd received from Peterson were just a coincidence.

I was startled back to the task at hand by a sharp knock on the hood of my Suburban. I jerked my head up and saw Ed Wynwood, Jr. give me a wave through the windshield, a grin spreading on his Basset-hound face. A veteran of the conflict in Afghanistan, he still kept his graying hair in a military cut. He wore a bright blue T-shirt with the outline of a spoon printed on it that represented the giant painted silver spoon on top of the small brick building that housed his diner. A grubby apron was tied around his waist.

"Got some goodies for me?" he asked when I stepped out.

"Sure do. How'd you know I was here?" Usually he didn't come out until I knocked at the back door to let him know I'd arrived.

Ed pointed to a camera mounted under the eaves. "Saw you on the monitor. Just put it up this week because someone was

43

getting into the dumpster and making a mess in the parking lot. How's the egg farming business?"

"Pretty good. How's the egg frying business?" I went around and opened up the back of the Suburban to unlock the egg cooler.

"Pretty good," he echoed. He nodded across the street, where Eli and Peterson had now ducked underneath the caution tape and were walking back and forth in front of the pump. Peterson waved his hands animatedly as he explained to Eli what had happened. Ed squinted at them. "You know what's going on over there? I saw them haul Homer off in an ambulance yesterday."

I nodded. "He passed on, I'm afraid."

Ed's face fell. "Sorry to hear that. Not too surprising, I guess. He wasn't exactly a healthy man."

"He had health issues?"

Ed nodded and pushed a kitchen cart over to the back of my car. "All that liquor is hard on your ticker. He carried some extra weight around his middle, too—I was always telling him to lay off the bacon. Me, saying 'cool it on the bacon,' can you believe it?" He shrugged and patted the not-small belly that threatened to spill over the top of his apron. "Maybe I should follow my own advice."

I chuckled as I loaded eggs onto his cart, my own stomach still stretched tight from the giant breakfast I'd put away earlier. "I should, too."

I held out my clipboard for Ed to sign and then tore off his part of the invoice. "Pay me when you can."

"Will do. Merry Christmas." Ed nodded and disappeared back into the tiny brick building with his cartload of fresh eggs.

Instead of getting back in the car, I headed over to the gas station. A one-pump wonder, Wilds Gas and Go had seen better days. The latest renovation seemed to have occurred in the Seventies. The psychedelic logo had faded so much that the colors were indistinguishable from one another, and the paint on the siding was peeling, revealing many layers of previous colors. I stood just outside the caution tape, unsure whether to step inside the boundary.

"He hit his head there." Peterson pointed to a spot on the metal pole that held up the roof over the pump. "Then he tripped and crashed into that." He indicated a concrete pillar meant to keep vehicles from crashing into the pump itself.

Eli squinted at the spots and jotted down notes as Peterson spoke. "So you didn't hit him at all?"

Peterson glanced guiltily at me and shook his head. "I maybe—"

"Maybe what?" Eli pressed.

"I mean, he was coming at me. I maybe pushed him away when he came too close." Peterson's hand went unconsciously to his injured eye. "I can't remember exactly—it all happened pretty fast."

"I see. And then what? How did it end?"

Peterson shrugged. "He ran out of steam, and I didn't stick around."

"He just walked back into his office?"

"I don't know. I didn't see. I just drove off. I don't know what you want from me." Peterson crossed his arms. I could tell his irritation was rising at the level of questioning, but his attitude wasn't helping his cause.

"Every detail is helpful," I said reassuringly. He glanced over at me and let out the breath he'd been holding, his shoulders

45

relaxing.

Eli nodded. "I'm just trying to construct a timeline. Did you see anyone else around who might be able to confirm your story?"

"No. I mean, maybe. I wasn't paying much attention to what was going on—I was so focused on getting to Leona." Peterson met my eyes for a long moment, pain flashing across his face. Between his tortured expression, fresh scratch, and gruesome shiner, I couldn't look away until Eli cleared his throat.

"I'll ask around town. Maybe someone noticed you stop for gas. Your car is pretty distinctive."

I scanned the blocks around the gas station. There were plenty of vantage points along the highway where people might have caught a glimpse of Peterson's car at the gas station—the florist, the dentist, the back lot of the diner where my Suburban was still parked. Usually nobody parked there except Ed himself, but sometimes people used it as a shortcut when they were walking by—or when they were dumpster-diving. *Hm.* Maybe the security camera caught something. If I squinted, I could just make out the camera attached to the building, and it was clearly angled in this direction.

I pointed across the street. "Ed has a camera now, and it's pointed this way. If he captured your stop on film, it'll clear everything up and you can go home." I shot Peterson a smile, expecting him to return it.

But he didn't. He stared across the street where I'd pointed like he didn't even see me.

"Good eye, Leona! I'll talk to Ed about it." Eli said. He planted a kiss on my forehead and clapped Peterson on the back. "Thanks for all your help, Pete."

Peterson—who usually bristled at any nicknames—gave him

a wan smile. "No problem."

It seemed to me there *was* a problem. Why wasn't he more enthusiastic about the idea being cleared of wrongdoing? Eli noticed, too. He paused, frowning. "You OK?"

Peterson snapped out of his trance with a little shake of his head. "Yeah—I'm fine. When you said I'd be able to head home, Leona, I just felt a little—I don't know. Sad." He gave me a small, apologetic shrug. "Home used to be with you."

Chapter 7

"I'll drop you off so you can spend some time with Andrea and the kids," I said, shifting the Suburban into gear. Since Peterson would soon be leaving, he probably wanted to get as much time with them as possible. After his heartfelt admission, I didn't want to rob him of a Christmas with his grandchildren. Maybe we could move up the celebration a few days so he wouldn't miss out on seeing them unwrap their presents. The kids were young enough that they didn't know what date it was, anyway.

"You're not staying?"

I eased the car to the edge of the parking lot and checked for cross-traffic. "I promised Ruth I'd help wrap the Gifting Tree donations. It's a big job, so they need as many hands as possible. I'll be back in time for dinner."

"Let me help," he said suddenly.

I raised an eyebrow. "You want to wrap gifts for charity?"

"Sure, why not?"

"I don't know—because you've never wrapped a gift in your life? When I did it myself for Andrea's first birthday, you literally hired a service and had all the gifts re-wrapped, remember?"

"I just wanted them to be nice for Andrea."

48

"They *were* nice." I sucked in my cheeks as I pulled out onto the highway and headed out of town, remembering all the care I'd put into choosing the paper, ribbons, and bows, not to mention the time it'd taken me. I tried and failed to keep the acid out of my tone. "She was one, Peterson. She didn't care about the paper. You know as well as I do that you wanted fancy packages to impress all the guests at the party—all those adults we barely knew that you invited to a baby's birthday so you could network."

"I know." His voice was low and guilty. I stole a peek at him in my peripheral vision and his face was somber as he stared at his hands in his lap. He raised his head. "I was wrong. And I want to make it up to you."

"One day won't make up for our whole marriage," I said, my eyes now trained studiously on the road so that my resolve not to cry wouldn't weaken. He was saying all the things I'd wanted to hear two years ago, but it was hard to believe he actually meant them.

"I'm not saying it will—I just want you to know that I'm sorry. Please, let me help you today?"

I braked and pulled into the sawmill parking lot, the last place to turn around before we hit the Curves. For the first time since we got in the car, I got a good look at Peterson. His face was earnest, pleading, even hopeful. He knew he didn't deserve forgiveness, but he wasn't too proud to ask for it.

"Fine—but you're going to have to text Andrea and tell her it was your idea to leave her stuck at the farm by herself with the kids all day. I don't want to be the bad guy."

"It's a deal." Peterson chuckled and pulled out his phone, speaking aloud as he typed while I made the turn and drove back in the direction we'd come. "Staying in town to help Mom.

We'll be home for dinner."

When we pulled up to the library where I was supposed to meet Ruth, her car wasn't there, but Gary's still-fully-decorated VW bus was. I parked next to it. Before I could get out, Peterson flashed his phone's screen toward me so I could read Andrea's reply to his message: "GREAT!!!!"

I giggled. "Four exclamation points? Wow, she really didn't want us there. Maybe she'd prefer not to see her parents at all this week."

Peterson chuckled. "My thoughts exactly."

The door to the community center was propped open, so we headed inside. The community center decorations were looking a little bedraggled after the first Honeytree Holidays gathering yesterday, but the Gifting Tree still stood tall and proud in the center of the room, the toys heaped around it. Ruth was bent over next to it, loading toys into a cardboard box, her face reddening with the effort. She stood up when she heard us come in and pushed her hair out of her face.

"Hi, Le—" She broke off when she saw Peterson beside me, her eyebrows nearly hitting her hairline.

"He came to help," I explained, suddenly self-conscious.

"Well, why not. Grab a box and fill 'er up." Ruth motioned to a few empty boxes beside her. "Gary couldn't help today because his daughters are visiting, but he loaned me his bus. Between that and your Suburban, I think we'll be able to do it in one trip."

Peterson grabbed two boxes and handed one to me. I ducked around to the other side of the tree and began stacking Barbie dolls and LEGO sets into my box while Ruth and Peterson worked to do the same. When I'd filled mine to the brim, I took it out to Gary's VW and slid it into the open cargo space. A dozen trips later, we'd loaded his bus with toys and crammed as many as could fit into my Suburban.

Ruth dusted her hands and grinned at both of us. "Many hands make light work, as they say."

"Where are we taking these?" I asked.

"Joan set up a wrapping assembly line at her shop," Ruth said. "Rusty's going to meet us there, and the Knitwits volunteered to help, too, so I think it's going to go really fast."

Joan owned a yarn and handicrafts shop called Knitty Gritty on a side street near the high school. The vast majority of her yarn business was online, and the shop itself mostly served as an unofficial clubhouse for the Knitwits, a group that met twice weekly to gossip and turn string into scarves and sweaters. They'd been the ones who knitted the charming miniature decorations for the Gifting Tree.

They also took on other charity projects throughout the year, whether it was knitting hats for women with breast cancer or blankets for children in the foster care system. Though the giftwrapping endeavor didn't involve yarn, I wasn't too surprised that the Knitwits were helping out with the Gifting Tree, since Joan was so involved with both organizations.

I shut the back doors of the Suburban and walked around to the driver's side. Peterson was already in the passenger seat, texting, when I slid behind the wheel.

"We're headed to the yarn shop to do the actual wrapping," I said to him. "You remember Mrs. Claus? She owns it. Runs it out of a cute little house over by the school."

He didn't seem to hear me. His thumbs worked furiously as he typed on the tiny phone screen.

"Who are you talking to?" I asked. I pulled out behind Ruth and followed the blinking Christmas lights on Gary's bus down the street, curiosity tugging at me. "Someone from the office?"

He sent the message he'd been typing and clicked off his phone. "Just giving Andrea an update," he said, looking out the window as I drove the few blocks over to the yarn shop, past the baseball field and the high school. He motioned to the red brick building. "Is that where you graduated?"

"Yep."

"It's like something out of a movie," he said. "So quaint. I can see why you love this little town. I honestly wish I'd visited sooner."

I turned down Mallow Lane and tried to swallow the bitterness that rose in my throat. It's not that I hadn't asked him to come here to Honeytree a hundred times while we were married. He'd always demur. "I shouldn't waste my vacation days," he'd say. "If I'm going to take time off work, I want to go somewhere good." Instead of visiting my hometown, we'd spend Christmas in Hawaii or on the beach in Mexico or under the Paris streetlights. He'd fly both our parents out, too. How could anyone complain about that? But I still missed my little hometown.

I parked next to Ruth just as Rusty pulled up. As soon as Ruth and I opened the back of our vehicles, we were surrounded by the Knitwits. The group—all female save one lone, graying gentleman—spanned every age and shape of womanhood, from a bespectacled teen with braces to elderly women who could be her great, great grandmother. They swarmed the stacks of toys, ferrying them into the little golden-brown Craftsman that housed Knitty Gritty like bees transporting pollen to their queen.

Inside, surrounded by shelves of yarn in every shade of the rainbow, Queen Joan presided over four long folding tables that had been set up in the center of the shop. Each table had a station for paper, ribbon, and tags so the gifts could be wrapped and labeled as quickly as possible. Joan delegated roles to everyone present, including the chore of choosing a gift out of the pile for each child on the Gifting Tree wish list.

Ruth, Rusty, Peterson and I weren't trusted with that enviable task—nor with the fine art of giftwrapping. Instead, we were assigned the grunt work: conveying wrapped packages to the appropriate bin in the back room for delivery on Christmas Day.

I manned the end of my assigned table, Ruth on my left and Rusty on my right. On the other side of Rusty, Peterson stood at attention, poised and ready to excel at the job. His competitive drive hadn't changed, whatever else had. He always wanted to be the best at everything. It was part of what attracted me to him initially, back when I was a college cheerleader and he was a fresh med school graduate. But it was also what had driven us apart. His high standards were too high for me, a wife who in many respects was only average.

The first wrapped package appeared in front of me. I checked the tag for the correct bin number and carried it to the sorting room. Peterson had already dropped his first gift and was heading back with a triumphant expression.

"You win," I said as we passed in the doorway.

He smirked at me. "What's my prize?"

Our amiable morning had given him way too much confidence. I rolled my eyes. "Don't get ahead of yourself. One package doesn't make Christmas, if you know what I mean."

"I guess I'll keep trying," he said, waggling his eyebrows. "Maybe by the end, you'll be more impressed with my package handling."

"Doubt it," I said, moving past him to the bins. I couldn't help breaking into a grin. His comment was so inappropriate, and I didn't intend to entertain it, but I couldn't help being a little flattered that he was flirting with me.

After Andrea moved to Chicago, it was like he didn't even see me…and when he did, it was to point out all the ways I could improve. His little suggestions over the years—*tone up a little, try a chemical peel, let me work my magic*—had whittled away my self-confidence to almost nothing. He'd always insisted they weren't a comment on my beauty or lack thereof, but it was hard to take them as anything but.

Maybe seeing me with another man had reminded him that I was still attractive. Eli didn't have a problem appreciating every ripple and curve I had to offer, and perhaps Peterson had caught a glimpse of me through his eyes. Well, he could still keep his comments to himself.

I returned to my station and found three wrapped gifts piled up at the end of the table. I'd better hustle if I was going to keep up with these busy elves. I picked up the pace, but Joan intercepted me as I balanced the three boxes on the way to the sorting area. She wore a green, handknit sweater with a turtleneck that threatened to swallow her head. In another life, it could have doubled as a Grinch costume.

"Careful you don't mix those up," she warned. "When you hurry, I worry. That's how mistakes are made. That's how things slip through the cracks. We don't want a child to be disappointed on Christmas morning."

"Of course not," I said quickly, scuttling past her and very nearly losing the top box in the process, earning me an extra glare. I paid special attention to the tag numbers as I sorted the packages, her watchful eye on my every move.

"Watch out for Mrs. Claus. She runs a tight workshop," Rusty whispered as he plunked a blue-and-silver gift with a glittery bow in the bin next to me. "Plus, the pay is terrible."

I giggled but quickly swallowed my amusement when I noticed Joan fixing us both with a disapproving stare. I spent the next hour running back and forth from the front room to the back, tuning out the chit-chat of the Knitwits at my table so I wouldn't get distracted and slow my pace or make an error. I was just feeling like Joan didn't hate me when a set of bells jangled on the front door of the shop. I looked up and saw Eli headed in my direction, his face grim.

"Bad news," he said when he reached me. The Knitwits at my table paused their assembly line to eavesdrop. Eli shot them an apologetic smile for the interruption, and they resumed their wrapping, although I could tell that some of them still had an ear cocked toward us. "Sorry to barge in—I saw your car parked out front and thought you'd want to know."

"Want to know what?" Peterson asked, abandoning his post to move over and stand next to me.

"I'm sorry to say, you're not out of hot water yet, Pete," Eli said. "I talked to Ed, and unfortunately he's not willing to turn over his security footage."

I stepped back, bumping into the growing stack of gifts that I should have already moved to the back room. "I don't understand."

"It's his choice at this point. I asked, he said no. That's that. I'm really sorry. It looks like you'll have to stick around at least until the autopsy report comes back," Eli added apologetically to Peterson.

I shook my head. Ed was such a rational, even-keeled guy. It seemed so odd that he wouldn't cooperate with a simple request from the sheriff. "Did he give you any reason?"

"He said he wasn't aware any crime had occurred. Until he knew otherwise, he felt it was best to protect everyone's privacy."

"Honorable," Peterson said at the exact same time I said, "Stupid."

When I felt both their eyes on me, I had to explain my choice of words. "What? It is stupid. That camera looks over a restaurant parking lot, a public street, and a gas station. It's not like it's anyone has an expectation of privacy in those places."

Eli nodded. "I agree with you on face. But Ed's within his rights to refuse."

"He's hiding something," I said. "There's something on that tape he doesn't want us to see."

"I'm not so sure about that. He said he'd hold onto the recording until after the autopsy report comes back. If it shows that Homer died of his injuries, then he'll turn it over to me. That'll give us a more accurate picture of what happened. Should confirm your story that he was alive and well when you left the gas station," he added to Peterson. "Unfortunately, you'll have to stick around until then. My guest room is open to you as long as you need it; I feel bad that you got mixed up in this."

Peterson stuck out his hand to shake Eli's. "Appreciate it, brother."

Brother? Were they in a fraternity now? Leona Sigma Chi? Well, at least Peterson wasn't starting another fistfight. Plus, as long as Eli was willing to play host, that meant Peterson wasn't staying at my house. No matter how nice he was acting, I still didn't want to be his roommate.

Chapter 8

Across the knitting shop, Joan cleared her throat meaningfully, and we all jumped to attention. The Knitwits redoubled their wrapping efforts, and I realized that the stack of boxes behind me had grown even higher. "Thanks for letting us know," I said to Eli. "I should get back to work."

"Santa's little helpers," he said bemusedly. "That's OK, I should, too."

I found myself in the sorting area at the same time as Ruth and Rusty as I scrambled to find the right location for my backed-up boxes.

"Were you talking about what happened to Homer?" Ruth asked me when we found ourselves in front of the same bin. "I heard about it last night. Terrible."

I tossed a small, purple-and-gold box into the pile. "Yep—unfortunately, Peterson stopped to fill up at the Gas and Go yesterday morning, and the two of them had a scuffle. He could be arrested if it turns out that Homer died from his injuries."

Ruth gave a small gasp. "I assumed it was alcohol-related!"

"It probably is. But until the medical examiner determines Homer's cause of death for sure, Peterson's stuck here in Honeytree."

Ruth's already wide blue eyes widened even further, and her hand flew to her mouth. "Oh my word! Rusty, did you hear that?"

Rusty sidled past her to add a gift to the bin just beyond her. "Yeah, so?"

"Didn't you have an interview for a job at the gas station yesterday?"

He shook his head and his cheeks flushed. "I was supposed to, but it didn't happen."

Ruth clicked her tongue in disappointment. "Too bad. I thought you might have seen something while you were at your interview that would help."

"Nope. Nobody wants to interview a crook like me, I guess." Rusty's blue eyes darkened and for the first time, I noticed a scar in his right eyebrow that hadn't been there before he left for prison. Though his sentence had been relatively short, it still couldn't have been easy serving those long months surrounded by hardened criminals. And coming back home to a place where everyone had *opinions* about you and your choices? Well, I knew exactly how much courage that took.

I put my hand on his arm. "Hey. Don't give up. The right door will open at the right time."

"That's true," Ruth agreed. "You're a hard worker and an honest person, and there's always a job for someone like that. You just have to be patient."

Rusty started to reply, but Joan swooped down like Oscar the Grouch with wings, interrupting him with a clap of her hands. "Wasting time is worse than stealing money!"

"Sorry, Joan!" Ruth chirped. "We just got distracted."

Another hour of hustle, and all the donated gifts had been wrapped and sorted. The Knitwits retrieved tins of cookies from their tote bags and set them out on the now-empty giftwrapping tables to share. Joan produced an electric kettle and opened a cupboard behind her cash register area to reveal a row of mugs hanging from small hooks, some labeled with names, above an assortment of herbal teas.

Once she'd helped herself, the Knitwits followed suit. Joan took a spot in a purple, overstuffed chair, a sugar cookie in one hand and a peanut butter cookie in the other as she beamed like a benevolent empress at the empty table that'd held all the gift donations. She ran a tight workshop, like Rusty said, but she sure got the job done. Well, with the help of a lot of us elves, anyway.

As several of the members got out their knitting and crochet projects and began adding rows to their colorful creations while others sat down to munch and sip, I got the feeling this was the format of their usual club meeting.

"Shall we get back to the grandkids?" Peterson asked me. He had a smile behind his eyes—I could see it even through the red-and-purple blotch and swelling.

"Sure. Let me say goodbye to Ruth first."

Ruth was pouring hot water into a mug with a teabag in it. "Orange gingersnap," she said. "Want some?"

"No, we're just leaving. I came to say goodbye."

"Aw, stay for cookies." When I shook my head, she pouted slightly. "Fine. See you at the Christmas in the Park tomorrow? Tambra's bringing her two. I bet they'd love to play with J.W. and Izzy."

Tambra, the manicurist who worked in Ruth's salon, was a single mom of two boys in first and third grade. Ollie and Dylan were sweet kids, but they were also bundles of kinetic energy that destroyed everything in their path and were usually

59

covered in dirt and something sticky. I tilted my head, doubtful that Andrea would approve of her well-behaved duo mixing with the likes of that wild pair.

"Oh, come on! The city rented a snow machine! Ed's going to run it for a few hours in the morning so there's a big pile to play in."

"Come on, Leona, you can't say no to a snowball fight." Peterson, tired of waiting by the door, had found me. His eyes sparkled—or at least the good one did. Now that I thought about it, the idea of pelting him with snowballs—all in good fun, of course—sounded very therapeutic.

"Ed Wynwood?" I asked Ruth. She nodded, and I was sold. The twins would have a blast, even if Andrea didn't thoroughly approve of their playmates...and maybe Christmas in the Park would afford me the opportunity to find out why Ed was so reluctant to let anyone see his security tapes. I could bend his ear while he was stuck manning the snow machine. "We'll be there," I told Ruth.

When Peterson and I got back to Lucky Cluck Farm, I made Andrea a cup of tea and took J.W. and Izzy out to the coop to give her a break. To my surprise, Peterson came with us.

"I won't let the chickens get them, if that's what you're worried about," I assured him, as he matched his pace to mine. "We're just going to collect eggs."

"No, I want to see your whole operation." He pulled his bomber jacket closed and zipped it up to his chin, then tucked his hands inside the shearling-lined pockets as the kids ran ahead of us. We crossed the driveway and made our way over to the chicken coop and run.

Peterson craned his neck to check out the weathervane on top. "I have to say, it's bigger than I thought it'd be. I pictured something a little more Clampett, a lot less Disney castle."

I giggled self-consciously. "Eli calls it my chicken palace. He helped me build it, though, so it's partly his fault."

Peterson cracked a smile and then his face grew serious. "He seems to be fond of you."

I flushed and handed him a wire basket that'd been hanging on the row of hooks on the end of the coop. I gave one each to J.W. and Izzy, too.

"How do *you* feel about *him?*" Peterson studied my face to see my reaction, but I ignored him. It was none of his business. Instead, I showed the twins how to open the nest box doors. Though they could reach the latch themselves, they were too short to see inside, so I hefted Izzy up high enough that she could collect the eggs.

"Ooh, pretty!" she exclaimed when she saw the clutch of eggs in the box. She grabbed the one nearest to us. It was a green one; though most of my hens were the typical brown layers, I had a few wildcards that had been included with my hatchery orders—they laid eggs that were blue, green, cream, and a brown so dark that it was almost red. I usually kept the rainbow eggs for myself and sold the brown ones to my egg customers.

Peterson wrinkled his nose and swiped the egg out of Izzy's hand before she could put it in her basket. "Ew, don't touch that. That's a rotten one."

"It's supposed to be that color," I said quickly, before he did something dumb like pitching it into the bushes. "It was laid in the last few hours, I swear. I check these boxes for eggs twice a day."

Peterson stared at the egg in his hand, turning it over to marvel at the pale green shell. Freckled with darker brown, it was a uniquely beautiful specimen, the kind you didn't even need to dye for Easter. "Huh. You learn something new every day."

J.W. tugged at my elbow. I let Izzy slide to the ground and held my arms out to him. "Do you want a turn?"

He gave a single, solemn nod, so I boosted him up to the nest box. He looped his basket over one sturdy little arm and went to work moving the remaining cluster of brown eggs into his basket with the focus of a seagull on a french fry. The last egg collected, I set him down and closed the door, latching it securely against predators. J.W. examined his basket contents and turned his big brown eyes on me. "Thanks, Nana."

My heart thrilled. They were the first words he'd spoken directly to me during the visit—or to any adult other than his mom. "Thank *you* for helping me with the farm chores."

"Can I go again?" Izzy asked.

"Yep, you can collect eggs until my arms wear out." I heaved her up to reach inside the next nest box.

"When's my turn?" Peterson joked.

I raised an eyebrow, frankly a little surprised that he wanted anything to do with the chickens after his experience with Boots in the bathroom. "Why don't you and J.W. take the other end, and we'll both work toward the middle?"

"As long as you promise that no wild hens are going to pop out and attack me." For a second, I thought he was serious, but then he cracked a smile.

"I'm the only wild hen around here, and you don't need to worry about me."

J.W. reached his little hand up and snaked it into Peterson's palm. "Come on, Gamp."

At the little boy's words, Peterson's breath caught. I knew

just what he was feeling, hearing his name come out of J.W.'s mouth. It was a gift. We exchanged a look over the top of the twins' heads, the kind only two doting grandparents can share.

If this was the only result of our marriage, these kids and this one moment, I couldn't help thinking that maybe it was all worth it.

Chapter 9

December 22

The roar of the snow machine as it spit a plume of white, frozen crystals into the air nearly drowned out the delighted squeals of Honeytree's children as they swarmed the park, tossing snowballs and sliding down the growing mountain of snow on garbage can lids. J.W. and Izzy stood transfixed in their matching red jackets, their mouths open, as they took in the scene.

Finally, Izzy let out her breath in a big huff. "This is awesome!" J.W. nodded in agreement.

Next to me, Andrea's expression said she felt otherwise. Her eyes roved the park, her eyebrows knitting anxiously as she watched a toddler in a pink snowsuit faceplant into a frosty pile. Peterson reached over and smoothed the lines in her forehead with his gloved hand. "Careful, or it'll stick like that. I've seen women with deep lines before forty because they're always pulling faces. I always say the best wrinkle treatment is prevention. The second best is Botox."

I elbowed him. "Knock it off. Her face is fine."

"It's OK, I know what he means," Andrea said. "I need to relax and stop being such a control freak. It's just hard. I can't really let the kids run wild in Chicago, so I'm not used to it."

"Can we please go play, Mama?" Izzy asked, her face turned up to Andrea. J.W. waited patiently beside his sister, his expression expectant.

I spotted Tambra and Ruth headed toward us, Tambra's boys in tow. I crouched down between J.W. and Izzy and pointed. "Look who's here! It's Ollie and Dylan. They can show you everything you need to know about Honeytree Park."

"Those are big boys," Izzy observed. "Are they nice ones or mean ones?"

"Nice. Also very funny." I shot Andrea a questioning look, and she gave a single nod.

"Put on your mittens," she reminded them. J.W. and Izzy dutifully slipped their hands into the mittens that dangled from their sleeves just as the boys and their mom reached us. I introduced Ollie and Dylan to the twins, and before I could blink, the four of them were scrambling over the piles of snow with the rest of the horde.

"I'm Peterson, Leona's husband," Peterson said.

"Ex," I interjected.

He pulled off his right glove and extended his hand to Tambra. "I have to say, whoever did your work was a master." I rolled my eyes. Tambra, a former Miss Oregon, was objectively gorgeous—but her beauty was all-natural, not the creation of some genius doctor.

She tossed her long red hair back behind her shoulders, her laugh filling the air as she shook his hand. "Why, thank you. I do my nails myself." She wiggled her fingers on her other hand to show off her silver, glittery polish.

I snorted. "He means your plastic surgery."

Ruth gave a loud laugh, jostling the cardboard tray of steaming hot cocoa in her hands. "Oh my gourd, Tambra, he thinks you've got fake—"

"She hasn't had any surgery," I said to Peterson. "But even if she had, you really shouldn't make comments like that."

"Sorry." He ducked his head, sheepish. Today, the swelling around his eye was down enough that it could open almost normally, but the purple part of the bruise had darkened to nearly black, and the red areas screamed out against his pale skin. With his cashmere scarf wound around his neck and the tip of his nose pinkened from the cold air, he looked a little bit like a snowman with one coal eye fallen out. "Professional interest," he explained apologetically.

"Well, I'll take it as a compliment. You know, you could really use a manicure," Tambra said, winking at him. "Professional interest."

Peterson gaped at her and then at the fingernails on his right hand, which were actually very tidy. I happened to know he got regular nail treatments back home. He quickly popped his glove back on to hide them.

"Just kidding," she said, smirking. Andrea and Ruth giggled.

Peterson's horrified expression switched to relieved and—if it could be believed—slightly embarrassed. Ruth rescued him by handing him a paper cup.

"Honeytree's finest instant cocoa, brewed by genuine Girl Scouts," she said. She handed Andrea the second one and I took the third. Ruth held the fourth out to Tambra.

"None for me." Tambra waved her glittery fingers. "I've already had too much sugar. The Pastry Palace is handing out free gingerbread and I had seconds."

"Is there any such thing?" Ruth took the last cup for herself, dropping the cardboard tray into the recycling bin nearby.

"As free gingerbread? Sure. On the table over there." Tambra nodded over to the other side of the park, where a covered picnic area hosted the Pastry Palace booth. In addition to the free gingerbread, they were selling decorated cookies to benefit the Gifting Tree. A long line stretched away from the table, inching slowly past the snow machine that was set up nearby.

"No, I meant as too much sugar." Ruth sipped her cocoa, her eyes twinkling under the wooly rainbow beanie she had pulled down over her forehead. That hat looked like something the Knitwits might make: chunky, cheap, and cheerful. She noticed me checking it out and smiled. "Do you like it? Joan sold it to me yesterday after you left. It's cute, except it gives me hat head." She pulled it partway off using the pompom on top to demonstrate how the snug fit had flattened her curls, then yanked it back down to her eyebrows.

"Worth the sacrifice for cuteness. It'll be great for our ski trip," I said. In lieu of exchanging holiday gifts, Ruth, Tambra and I had gone in on a ski cabin rental up near Diamond Lake. We had a girls' weekend scheduled for mid-January that was going to be the highlight of the year. "Hey, does anyone else want gingerbread? I'm going to go stand in line." Truthfully, I was eager to see if I could get Ed to open up a little more and find out what he might be hiding on the security footage, and the slow-moving line near the snow machine was the perfect excuse.

Ruth instantly raised her hand, and Tambra shook her head *no*.

"Me." Andrea answered with her eyes still trained on the twins, who'd made it all the way to the top of the snow "mountain" with help from Dylan and Ollie. "Dad, how about you?"

"I'll come with you," Peterson said to me. "You might need some extra hands to bring it back."

I shrugged. I was confident I could manage an armload of gingerbread, but if he wanted to fetch and carry, I wasn't going to argue. We crunched across the snow to the end of the line, several yards behind the snow machine. I tried to catch Ed's eye, but he was fully absorbed in snowflake production.

Though the machine itself was cordoned off by orange plastic fencing, groups of kids kept pressing too close and stepping on the water supply hose that ran from the faucet in the picnic area to the back of the machine. Every so often he had to shoo them away so the snow could keep flying out of the machine's wide, roaring fan.

"Do you know him?" Peterson asked, noticing my interest. Knowing him, he probably thought Ed was another man I'd dated.

"Yep. One of my biggest egg customers. That's the guy who owns the restaurant across the street from the gas station—the one with the camera." Ahead of us, Ed hit a button on the control unit. The noisy fan in the snow machine died down.

"That's it! Snowstorm's over," Ed announced cheerfully, sweeping his arm to indicate the huge pile of snow that the machine had generated. The kids close enough to hear him groaned in chorus, but quickly resumed their gleeful antics. Ed moseyed over to the picnic area and unplugged the machine from a heavy-duty extension cord, then wrapped the cord around his arm as he retraced his steps. It looked like he was stowing the machine and readying it for return to the rental outfit.

"Motherclucker," I muttered, mentally willing the line to

move faster so we could reach Ed before he finished his task.

"What is it? If you didn't bring enough money, I can get it." Peterson slipped his wallet out of his inside jacket pocket and held it out to me, blocking my view.

I swiped it away, irritated. "The gingerbread's free, Peterson. Some things you can't fix with a wave of your magic wallet."

With an injured look, he tucked his wallet away and zipped his jacket up to his chin, then stuffed his hands in his pockets like a sulky child. "Well, if you'd just tell me what was bothering you, I might be able to help. Nobody can read your mind, so you can't get mad at us for guessing."

Us? Who else was he talking about?

I turned to him, puzzled. "You're the only one standing here, as far as I can see."

"From what Eli says, you make him work pretty hard, too. He never knows how you really feel, because you always keep him at arm's length."

The words hit me like a punch in the stomach. I opened my mouth to snap back, but nothing came out. I was genuinely speechless, for once.

Peterson shrugged at my dumbfounded expression. "We had a long talk last night. It was surprisingly nice to chat with someone who's been there, done that."

By *that*, I could only assume he meant me. I started to grumble at the characterization, but the line finally moved, and I obediently stepped forward. Out of the corner of my eye, I glimpsed Ed drifting away from the snow machine. He'd covered it with a large orange tarp, and it looked like he was heading toward the parking area.

I felt a surge of panic. Was he leaving? He probably had to get back to the diner to prepare for the dinner rush. As annoyed as I was to hear that Peterson and Eli were bonding over their shared complaints about me, I didn't have time to litigate the situation. My chance to talk to Ed was evaporating.

"You get the gingerbread," I ordered Peterson. "I'll be right back." I left the line before he could object, cutting across the hill of snow to catch up with Ed. It was larger and steeper than I'd anticipated at first glance, and I huffed, puffed, and slid my way across, dodging children and the occasional unleashed dog that cavorted in the drifts on either side of the sliding area. I had to jog the last few yards to reach Ed before he got into his truck.

"Hey, Ed!" I skidded to a stop in front of his front fender, bracing my hands on my thighs to catch my breath. He looked up and seemed to notice me for the first time.

"What's up?" He swung his car keys around his finger and caught them, once, twice, three times.

Unfortunately, I hadn't quite worked out what to say to him. I held up a finger, pretending I still hadn't caught my breath. "One sec."

What did I really hope to find out by questioning him? Of course, I was dying to know why he didn't want anyone to see those security tapes. His excuse about privacy was bunk—I knew that. The fact that he was willing to turn them over once it was clear a crime had occurred was a flimsy justification. At that point, Eli would be able to get a warrant to compel him to turn over the tapes, so it wasn't a mark of Ed's good character that he was volunteering them.

"I really need to get back to the diner," Ed said, his tone apologetic.

"It's about Homer," I blurted out. "I thought, since you two were neighbors for so many years, you might want to say a few words at his memorial service."

Ed frowned. "Is something planned? I hadn't heard about it."

I winced. I really should have thought this through. "Well, not *planned* planned. But if you want to throw your name in the hat now, I'm sure you'd get dibs on delivering the eulogy, since you guys had such a close relationship. You probably have a lot of nice things to say about him."

Ed dropped his keys mid-swing. He stooped to pick them up and unlocked the truck door before he answered me. It seemed I wasn't the only one stalling for time. "I'm—I'm not sure I'm the right person to do that," he stuttered.

I played dumb, trying to keep my voice level even though my heart was pounding. "Why not? Did something happen between you?"

Ed looked past me to where the kids were playing in the magical winter wonderland he'd created. He bunched his lips thoughtfully as he stared into the distance. "I wouldn't say that. We just had a little disagreement, and I wish we'd left things differently." His eyes focused back on me and he gave a sad smile. "Ah, well, it's too late now. You never know when someone's going to make their exit, so you gotta butter their bread while you can reach their plate, if you know what I mean."

With a goodbye nod, he swung into his truck and pulled out. As I watched him drive away, I mulled over what Ed had revealed. He and Homer, they'd had *some* kind of disagreement—one that hadn't been resolved before Homer died. I didn't know exactly what happened between them, but it sure sounded like a possible motive for murder to me.

Chapter 10

I was surprised to see Eli's SUV waiting in the driveway when we returned to the farm. He waved at us through the windshield as Andrea pulled her rental car up beside him. He held up a bottle of champagne and pointed to it, a huge grin on his face. I wondered what we were celebrating... and why he'd driven here instead of just walking over from his house.

"I might need a hand," Peterson said from the back seat, chuckling. I turned to see what he was talking about. Two little heads lay on Peterson's shoulders, bookending him where he sat wedged between their booster seats. J.W. and Izzy had fallen asleep on the short drive home, exhausted by their snowy adventures in the park.

Andrea and I got out and opened the doors to the back seat to unload the kids, but Eli lassoed me into a hug before I could lift Izzy to take her inside. I could feel the chill of the champagne bottle pressed against the small of my back as he pulled me close. "I have great news," he murmured against my neck. He planted a swift kiss on my ear and released me, grinning when he saw the blush that had crept up my cheeks.

"Can you get the front door?" I asked him as I ducked into the car to unclip Izzy's seatbelt. I scooped her up, grateful that my daily farm chores had strengthened my biceps so I was equal to the task. I left the car door open so Peterson could get out and followed Andrea up the front steps. Eli dashed ahead of us, taking the stairs two at a time, and pushed the door open so Andrea, with J.W. in her arms, could enter.

"Aren't you curious why I came straight from work?" Eli asked as I passed him in the doorway.

I kept my voice low so I wouldn't wake the twins. "Dying to know. Let me stow the passenger and you can tell me all about it."

The steep stairs to my attic bedroom with an extra forty-five pounds in my arms nearly did me in, but I made it to the top of the stairs and, feeling triumphant, laid Izzy down on the bed next to her brother. She made a drowsy noise of complaint but quickly settled back into a deep sleep. J.W. moved closer to her, throwing an arm over her shoulders.

"They always sleep like that," Andrea whispered next to me. "Even when I put them to bed in their own rooms, nine times out of ten, they end up snuggled up together by morning."

I clutched my chest to demonstrate the deluge of sweetness that flooded my heart. They were such dolls. "You and Steve are doing a great job with them, Andrea," I whispered back. "I'm so proud of you."

To my surprise, tears welled in Andrea's eyes. She blinked them away, swallowing hard. Something I'd said had touched a nerve.

"What is it?"

She shook her head and pasted on a smile, though there was little happiness evident behind it. "Nothing. I just wish Steve were here."

I gave her hand a sympathetic squeeze. It had to be tough

73

solo-parenting twins, especially away from home, without all their usual toys and routines. "He's flying in tomorrow, right?"

She pressed her lips together and shook her head, and a rogue tear escaped, tumbling down her cheek. "He's not coming. He texted this morning."

"Shoot." I pulled her into a hug, and she snuffled against my shoulder. With my arms still wrapped around her, I asked, "Did something come up at work?"

Steve's job as a cardiologist at one of Chicago's busiest heart clinics meant he worked long, odd hours and was often on-call at the local hospital, too, even on weekends and holidays. When he did have time at home, he was usually exhausted or asleep, and his planned vacation days didn't always pan out. Andrea had to be very flexible to accommodate Steve's unpredictable schedule. It wasn't much different than being in a relationship with a law enforcement officer, I reflected.

"No." Andrea's voice was so quiet I almost couldn't make out the word. "He just doesn't want to come. He's going to his parents' in Winnetka."

"Oh, hon." I pulled away to see her face, smoothing back a lock of blonde hair that was stuck to her teary cheek. "Don't worry about it. Not everybody wants to hang out with their mother-in-law on the farm."

For some reason, that made her cry harder. "It's not you, Mom," she choked out, forgetting to whisper. "It's me! I've been restless lately and asking a lot of him, and he says it's too much."

"You're not too much," I said firmly. "You're just right."

"Hard to believe when my own husband needs a break from me. I know he gives everything to his work, but I'm so lonely at home with the kids all day, Mom. When he doesn't even have the energy to listen to me, it feels like I've lost my best friend." Her voice cracked on the last word.

The sound of her voice roused Izzy, who shifted in the bed, grumbling restlessly, though her eyes were still closed. Andrea ducked her head guiltily and motioned downstairs.

I nodded and tiptoed behind her. When we reached the bottom, she caught my arm. "Don't tell Dad that Steve and I are having problems, OK? I don't want him to think that I'm"—she hiccupped and lost her breath momentarily, then recovered—"that I'm not trying hard."

"He wouldn't think that." I squeezed her hand again, my heart squeezing even harder at the thought of my sweet girl suffering in silence. "We can talk more later, OK? After Dad and Eli leave." She gave a nod and I let her hand go just as the *pop* of a champagne cork sounded in the kitchen.

"That's my name, don't wear it out," Andrea joked as she tried to clean up her face with her sleeve. I handed her a Kleenex from a box behind the couch and she blew her nose noisily before we headed into the other room.

When we got there, Eli handed us each a flute of sparkling wine. He and Peterson held tumblers of the same; I only had two champagne flutes in my limited kitchen cupboard space. I knew it had to be driving Peterson crazy to drink out of the wrong-shaped glass, so I silently switched with him.

"What are we toasting to?" I asked, giving Andrea cover so she could drop her soggy tissue into the trash.

"The inside scoop." Eli's chest puffed out slightly as he explained. "The official report won't drop until tomorrow, but your man on the inside"—he pointed to himself—"heard from his contact at the medical examiner's office that...*drumroll please...*Homer's death wasn't due to his injuries from the fight! You're off the hook, Pete!" Eli clinked his glass against Peterson's flute, who was standing next to him, dumbfounded, and then raised it to meet my tumbler.

I toasted automatically, a swirl of emotions in my chest. It was good news—great news, even. Peterson wouldn't have any legal trouble here in Oregon, which meant he could drive back to L.A. tomorrow. That's what I wanted, wasn't it? A return to normalcy. A peaceful Christmas on my little farm with my daughter and grandchildren, no uninvited guests turning up on the front porch.

So why didn't I feel happier about it?

A glance at Andrea revealed that she had mixed feelings, too. And Peterson was dead quiet as he sipped from his champagne glass. Eli stared around the room, puzzlement etched on his face. "I have to admit, I was expecting a little more enthusiasm about this news."

"No, it's great," Andrea assured him. I wondered if he noticed her red-rimmed eyes above the toothy smile she shot in his direction. "Thanks so much for all your help, Eli. You've been so kind and warm to our family."

"Peterson's not—" I started to say *not my family anymore* but thought better of it. I swallowed my words and took the sentence in a different direction. "Not leaving right this second, though. It's too late to start such a long drive. Is it OK if he stays with you until tomorrow, Eli?"

"Of course."

Peterson, who'd been completely silent until now, cleared his throat. "Well. I am relieved. Thank you, Eli. Andrea said it so well; your hospitality has been downright overwhelming. Especially considering"—his eyes flicked to me, and then back to the floor—"how it could have gone."

Now that he was leaving, I felt a pang of guilt at giving him such a frosty welcome. Though I'd divorce him all over again—he hadn't changed *that* much—I'd realized over the past couple of days that Peterson had come to Honeytree with the best intentions. He wanted to spend time with Andrea on her terms, which meant bringing all of us together. I couldn't fault him for that.

"Why don't we move up Christmas?" I said, feeling rash.

"What do you mean, Mom?"

"Let's do it tomorrow, so we can celebrate together. Christmas dinner, opening presents, the whole nine yards. It'll only mean staying one extra day." My voice rose questioningly at the end of the statement, and I met Peterson's eyes, hoping to show him that my invitation was genuine. He gave a slow nod, and I turned back to Andrea. "The kids won't mind getting their gifts a little early, will they?"

She chuckled. "No, they won't mind at all."

"Well. I'll be going," Eli said gruffly, setting his tumbler in the sink. Something about the way he carried his shoulders was off—he seemed tense, the joy he'd had when he'd passed out the glasses of champagne gone from his posture.

"Stay for dinner," I said, but he shook his head, his smile tight as he moved toward the front door.

"Don't want to interrupt your family time."

I frowned slightly and, with a quick, apologetic look at Andrea, tagged after Eli as he grabbed his coat. I followed him out on the porch and closed the door behind us so we could speak without being overheard. Though it wasn't yet five o'clock, the sky had already darkened considerably, and the air was chill. Judging by the quiet mutters from the chicken coop, the hens had already put themselves to bed.

"It's fine, Leona." Eli spoke before I could say anything. "I'm fine. I'm a big boy; I can make my own dinner."

"I know you are." I ran my hand down his uniform shirt front, the buttons bumping under my palm as I smoothed the khaki fabric. "A very handsome, very big boy."

He made a face. "Now you're teasing me."

"I'm not. I'm serious. I just...I don't want you to feel left out, that's all. You're my—" I broke off. I couldn't say family, not exactly. "You're my person," I finished lamely.

He leaned down and kissed my forehead, but he didn't say anything for a long minute. Then he took a deep breath and let it out in a blast. "Pete and I have been talking and—"

I groaned, slumping into his chest. "Don't listen to anything he says! He saw me at my worst, Eli. I was so stupid and broken—you have no idea. But I swear, that's not who I am anymore. I mean, I know I'm crabby sometimes, and I don't always let you in, but I *want* to. I want you to feel safe with me, as safe as I feel with you." I stopped, suddenly conscious that I was babbling.

A smile quirked the corner of his mouth, then disappeared. "What I was trying to say is that you weren't the only one injured in the divorce. Pete has a lot of regrets, and you two share a daughter. You share grandchildren. You shared decades as partners. I can't consider myself an equal in this equation just because I love you. I need to step back while you sort things out with him. See what comes of a reconciliation, OK? See what your family looks like when you put the pieces back together."

"What? No!" I grabbed his arm as he turned to go. "Don't be crazy. I'm not getting back together with Peterson."

"He has a lot to offer you, Leona." Eli stared down at his boots.

78

I snorted. "Did he tell you that? Then I've got a hen that lays golden eggs to sell you."

"I'm serious. A big house, fancy cars, vacations around the world." He gestured to the cottage. "Plus a happy family. Anything you want, you can have with him. I can't give you any of that."

"Yeah, but you have blueberries. He doesn't have blueberries."

"Be serious," he chided.

"I am being serious. I had all that stuff for way too long. It sucked. I hated it. You know where I came instead? Back here to Honeytree. To be with you."

This time he couldn't stop his smile. "You didn't want me around, remember? I distinctly recall you telling me to get off your property. More than once."

I giggled in spite of the serious topic at hand. "I told you—I was stupid and broken then. It took being here, being around you and Ruth and everyone to put myself back together again. To remember who I was and what I wanted out of life." I stood on tiptoes to steal a quick kiss, mostly to reassure myself, and then settled back down on my heels. "I don't want fancy, I don't want fuss, I don't want Christmas in Paris. I'm a simple girl who wants a simple life on my little farm next door to a hot blueberry farmer. That's it, OK?!"

"OK. I can't argue with that." He chuckled, shaking his head. "You know, Pete's right about you."

My heart sank. "I thought we just agreed that I've improved since then."

"When we were talking last night, he told me that it was no use trying to fit you into a box. He said no matter how long you stayed in it, eventually you were going to bust out, so I shouldn't even try."

OK, so maybe Peterson had learned something from our marriage after all. "Stay for dinner?" I pleaded.

Eli shook his head firmly. "Not tonight. But tomorrow, if you're open to it and you don't think Andrea and Pete will mind...?"

"Yes. I want you to come. It won't be a real Christmas without you."

"Then I'll be there."

Chapter 11

December 23

The next morning flew by in a blur of grocery shopping and farm chores. After lunch, Andrea and I took turns wrapping gifts at the kitchen table and getting the dinner prepped while Peterson did his best to keep up with the twins outside. He must have made a dozen laps around the house, following J.W. and Izzy as they chased the flock of chickens, before he collapsed on an Adirondack chair to watch them from the porch.

Andrea grinned out the window at them while she peeled sweet potatoes in the sink. "Does your house chicken eat potato peelings, or should I throw these out?" she asked, turning to me.

"Compost," I said automatically. I stuck a red bow on top of the present I'd been wrapping and paused. I hadn't seen Boots all day. Usually she sat on my lap while I drank my coffee, begging for breakfast crumbs, but with the twins around, I hadn't been doing too much sitting. "Did Boots sleep in your room last night?"

"No, why?"

I frowned. She hadn't slept on her usual perch on the back of the recliner, either. In fact, I didn't recall seeing her since a certain bathroom incident with a certain ex-husband a few days ago. It wasn't too uncommon for Boots to disappear every once in a while, when she decided to spend a night on the roost in the coop with her sisters. But three days in a row? She'd never stayed away from the house that long before.

I stood up from the table. "I need to go check on the chickens."

Andrea nodded absentmindedly, humming to herself as she sliced the peeled sweet potatoes and arranged them in careful rows in a baking dish. I slid my boots on and grabbed a jacket on my way out the door, blowing past Peterson on the porch as I clomped out into the yard.

Alarm Clock noticed me right away, chirruping from his perch on top of one of the fence posts near the orchard. The group of hens that J.W. and Izzy had been chasing heard his alert call and veered toward me. The rest of the flock stopped their grazing in the cropped green grass under the apple trees and swiveled their heads in my direction.

"Chick-chick! Come get a treat!" I called. Though I didn't have the bag of dried mealworms in my hand, the chickens seemed persuaded to at least investigate my offer. As the birds crowded around me, pecking hopefully at the toes of my boots and every speck on the ground, I scanned the flock for any sign of Boots. She was a little red layer, like the vast majority of my hens, but I could usually tell her apart by her slightly crooked toes and the colored zip tie around her left leg.

She wasn't there. The chickens lost interest when I didn't produce any actual treats and began to disperse. The loud song of a hen who'd just laid an egg caught my ear. Of course—Boots was probably just holed up in one of the nest boxes, working on her daily delivery.

To keep up the flock's production during the chilly, dark winter months, I'd installed a low-wattage heater and a light on a timer inside the coop; so far, instead of the steep drop expected this time of year, my hens were still laying about ninety-five percent their usual rate. Boots was likely attracted to the warmth and heat rather than laying her egg in her favored summertime spot, the planter of pansies on the back porch, or her favored winter spot, the laundry hamper.

But a quick check of the nest boxes proved me wrong. The only hens still on the nest were my two ditzy Polish girls, Phyllis and Cher, who were both wedged into a single box. When I opened the door, they clucked at me, their ridiculous sprays of head feathers bobbing with indignance. It wasn't their fault they couldn't see through their own hairdos.

"It's just me, ladies," I reassured them. They settled, so I closed up the door and leaned against the coop, thinking. Maybe Boots had gotten stuck in the barn when I moved my Porsche back in there.

But a thorough search of the barn proved fruitless, and I was out of ideas. Boots was officially missing. Instantly my mind went to the worst-case scenario. Maybe she'd drowned in a ditch. Maybe a stray dog had swiped her off the porch when I was in town. Maybe a hawk had swooped down and carried her off. Or maybe...

My gaze lifted to the porch, where Peterson was busy looking at his phone and ignoring J.W. and Izzy. They were still after the chickens and had made it halfway to the highway, I now saw—way too far for them to stray without adult supervision.

I cupped my hands around my mouth and yelled down the driveway at them. "That's far enough! Come back!"

J.W. and Izzy stopped in their tracks and reversed course, their breath sending up soft plumes of fog into the air as they ran back toward me. I made a mental note to compliment Andrea on her parenting again. It wasn't every four-year-old that would listen the first time you told them something. But first, I had some scolding to do.

I mounted the porch steps to stand in front of Peterson, my hands planted on my hips. Despite my call to the twins, he hadn't lifted his eyes from the screen. I cleared my throat and he glanced up.

"What? I was watching them."

"Sure you were. What if they kept going toward the road? They were too far for you to catch up."

"They didn't," he said mildly. He checked his phone again, and I growled with irritation.

"Only because I caught them before they disappeared. Speaking of disappearance..." I tapped my foot on the porch floor until he looked up again. "Where's my chicken, Peterson?"

"Which one?" He gestured to the orchard, where my flock was spread out beneath the bare-branched apple trees, scratching in the grass to stir up any bugs that hid between the frosty blades.

"You know which one. Boots. I haven't seen her since you scared her in the bathroom. What did you do to her?"

"*It* scared *me*. How do you know it's not out there with the other ones, anyway? It's not like you can tell them apart." He slid his phone into his inner jacket pocket and stood up, rubbing his hands together. "I'm cold; I'm going inside."

"Sure, just walk away," I said bitterly. "Leave your grandchildren unsupervised. I'm sure it'll be fine."

He rolled his eyes and made a dismissive gesture, moving

toward the door. Over his shoulder, he said, "They're not unsupervised; you're watching them."

I flung out my hands in frustration. "This is _so_ typical. I tell you there's a problem you need to solve, and you walk away and say I should fix it myself."

He turned around, his mouth tight. "I can't be one hundred percent responsible for your happiness, Leona," he spat. "Not anymore."

If my anger had been simmering before, now it heated into a rolling boil. "Since when did that ever happen?!" I screeched. "I gave up everything for you. I shaped my entire life around your career and your preferences. Where to live, what to eat, who to _be_—you chose it all. My happiness had nothing to do with it."

"Exactly," he said, his voice clipped and bitter. "You got to complain about every single thing, because you weren't responsible for any of it. I had to guess what would make you happy, and I always guessed wrong."

"That's because you didn't know me. You didn't know my heart, because you never cared to know. You never asked me who I was because the answer might have gotten in the way of your _plans_. Admit it." I stared at him, unblinking. "You cast me in a role that I had to play, and it was your way or the highway. Surprise, surprise, eventually I chose the highway. The open road will always beat a locked garage, no matter how expensive the décor is inside."

He stared back at me for a brief, silent moment and then whirled and went back in the house, banging the door shut behind him. _My_ house. Suddenly I wished I'd kicked him out this morning and hadn't offered to rush together this whole fake Christmas. He didn't deserve it. He hadn't learned anything.

"Nana, let's play a game!" Izzy said breathlessly from the bottom of the steps behind me.

I pushed down my anger and turned to smile at her. "What kind of game?"

"You be the sheep and we'll be the wolves," J.W. said eagerly, his cheeks and nose ruddy from the chill air. It seemed their adventures chasing chickens had just been a warm-up for the main event.

"OK, let me work on my accent." I bleated a few times to get into character. But before I could join them at the bottom of the steps, my phone buzzed in the back pocket of my jeans. With a guilty look toward the house, since I'd just chastised Peterson for doing the same, I checked it. It was a text message from Ruth with one word: "HELP!"

"You know what, guys? Before we play wolves and sheep, let's go inside for a cookie." I shooed the twins back into the house and helped them with their shoes and coats, releasing them to Andrea for a snack before I called Ruth to see what was going on.

"Are you OK?" I asked when she picked up. I headed for the guest bedroom, pretending I didn't notice Peterson sitting on the sofa as I walked through the living room. It was quieter in the guest room, plus I could check around for Boots while I talked to Ruth.

She gulped a huge breath. "I know you have a house full of guests, but is there any chance you can abandon your family and help me for a few hours? Ugh, even just saying it, I know the answer. Of course you can't, you have a house full of company. I'm sure you already have plans."

"What's going on?" I got down on my hands and knees on

the rag rug next to the bed to check behind the dust ruffle. A lone red feather lay on the bare floor beneath the bedsprings.

A chill skittered up my spine. It felt like an omen. I shook it off and turned my attention back to the phone conversation. "I assume this is about the Honeytree Holidays somehow?"

"You assume right." Ruth gave another big sigh. "It's a long story, but basically the Gifting Tree Committee was supposed to provide refreshments for the Walk-Thru Nativity tomorrow, but Joan called me up today to tell me that they're not doing it."

"What? Why not?"

"She said their donation level was too low this year. They needed the refreshment budget to fulfill all the kids' requests."

"Bummer," I said thoughtfully. I stood up from the floor and rubbed my stiff knee joint before moving to check in the closet. It was closed, but maybe Andrea had accidentally left it ajar when she stowed her suitcases in there. I peeked inside—no Boots, but I spied a pile of wrapped gifts. Of course, Andrea had been thoughtful and organized enough to wrap them all before she came. "Did you ask Pastor Cal if the church can come up with something?"

"They're tapped out, too—they spent their whole budget on renting camels for the Wise Men."

I laughed out loud as I shut the closet door. "I had no idea camels were available for rent!"

Ruth didn't share my amusement. "Yeah, and they're not cheap. Anyway, now I've got to rustle up some last-minute donations, and I was *hoping* maybe you could help me this afternoon and call the rest of the businesses in the Chamber of Commerce to see if they'll pitch in. Any chance you can take half the list?"

I checked the time. With all the prep Andrea and I had done

already, there wasn't much to do in the kitchen except put everything in the oven. The cranberry sauce was chilling in the fridge, the ham was ready to go in the oven, the potatoes and sweet potatoes had been peeled and cut up, the green beans were trimmed. I could spare some time—especially if it was time I didn't have to talk to Peterson.

"I'll do it. What kind of donations are you looking for?"

"I'll take anything edible—we're selling snacks and drinks to fund next year's Honeytree Holidays. Or money. Money is always good. With money, we can buy snacks and drinks."

"Got it. Email me my half of the list."

Ruth gave a sigh of relief. "You're an angel, Leona. I mean it."

And for a second, I really did feel that halo over my head.

Chapter 12

The halo came crashing down around my shoulders the instant I stepped out of the guest room. There was Peterson on the couch, glued to his phone, typing away with his thumbs, oblivious to Izzy and J.W. who were trying to get his attention by untying the laces on his oxfords.

Andrea swooped by, steering the twins away from him. "Don't bug Gamp. He's doing important stuff."

It broke my heart. I felt like I was watching Andrea's childhood play out all over again—except this time it was her kids being ignored and Andrea making the excuses instead of me. I wanted to scream at him to wake up! He was missing out on moments he wasn't going to get back! But my phone alerted me that Ruth had sent the Chamber of Commerce list, so I left him to rot on his keister and followed Andrea back to the kitchen.

"Do you mind getting dinner in the oven?" I asked apologetically. "I need to step out for a bit."

Andrea lowered her voice and drew me over to the side of the kitchen so the kids wouldn't overhear. "Are you mad at Dad again? I saw how you were looking at him out there."

She seemed so miserable that I couldn't tell her the truth. "Something just came up with one of the community events, and I need to make some calls. I promise, I will be nice to him tonight. We're going to have a happy Christmas, all of us together."

I'd fake it if it killed me. It was the least I could do for her and the kids. We'd end his visit on a good note and then in the morning, he'd vanish back to Southern California where he belonged and the rest of us would have some *real* fun.

She shot me a relieved smile, and I bundled up and headed out to the porch to cold-call half the businesses in Honeytree. An hour later, I had a short but bountiful list of donations. The Pastry Palace volunteered ten pumpkin pies, the Rx Café offered five cranberry cheesecakes, and Ed promised fifteen dozen cinnamon-sugar donuts from the Greasy Spoon's deep-fryer if I'd pick them up in the morning and deliver them myself.

When I texted Ruth with my successes, she sent me a whole screen of hearts, then added, "Great! The grocery store is going to donate two boxes of oranges and a big urn of coffee, and Shelly says she has a ton of extra poinsettias that we can have if they're not sold by tomorrow afternoon." Shelly was the woman who ran the florist shop. Ruth had really called everyone in the Chamber. Another message zipped in beneath the last. "The insurance office gave me a check so we can buy drinks. What else should we get besides creamer for the coffee?"

I didn't even have to think before I texted back. "Save the $$ for next year. Lucky Cluck Farm will donate twenty gallons of apple cider."

"Are you sure? Never mind, don't answer that—we'll take it." Ruth added a few hearts and a Mrs. Claus emoji after her message. After we arranged to meet at the church in the morning, I tucked my phone away, bracing myself for what awaited me inside.

"Keep it together for Andrea," I said under my breath as I opened the door. "It's not forever. One more night, and he'll be gone."

Peterson rose to his feet when he spotted me heading for the kitchen. "Are you still—"

"No," I cut him off, holding up my hand. "Everything's fine."

He stepped into the doorway between me and the kitchen, blocking my path. I stopped short, eyeing the mistletoe above his head warily. "Fine, or *fine*? Because sometimes when you…" He trailed off, seeming to think better of what he was about to say. "I wasn't sure whether or not you were still giving me the silent treatment, that's all."

I made a face at him, careful to stay out of the mistletoe zone. "It's Christmas. Let's do our best to be nice to each other for the next twelve hours or so. Then we never have to see each other again."

Peterson nodded slowly, the dark ring around his left eye making him look like a guilty hound dog. I started to edge my way around him into the kitchen, but a gentle rapping at the front door caught both our attention.

Before I could go answer the knock, the door cracked open and Eli stuck his head inside. His eyes immediately flicked up to the doorframe above our heads and widened. I remembered a beat too late that Peterson and I were standing *very* close together under the mistletoe. I'd entered the zone without realizing it. I grimaced and hastily backed up.

"Ho, ho, ho!" Eli said, pushing the door all the way open and brandishing an armload of gifts. They were wrapped in plaid paper that closely matched the flannel shirt he wore under his open jacket.

I grinned at him. "Very color-coordinated."

He looked down at his outfit and chuckled. "What do you know—I didn't even plan it."

"Let me put those under the tree." Peterson took the packages from Eli, who seemed hesitant to relinquish them, and nestled them under one side of the Doug fir that temporarily inhabited the far corner of the living room.

I'd cut the tree myself from the edge of my property, so it didn't have the perfect, groomed look of a tree for sale on a professional Christmas tree lot. The trunk was slightly crooked and it was missing a few branches. But I'd put the flat side against the wall and draped it in colorful lights and all of the ornaments Andrea had created in her youth—the cut-and-paste, yarn-wrapped, glitter-glued glory that Peterson had never let us display on our "real" tree—and the tree gave my living room the cheerful homemade look that I loved.

The base of the tree was now overflowing with gifts. While I was upstairs making calls, Andrea must have added the ones she brought from Chicago to the presents we'd wrapped this morning, and Peterson had contributed a load of professionally wrapped boxes that he must have had stowed in his car for the drive up to Oregon. It was shaping up to be a real Christmas.

I felt a slight pang that I hadn't gotten anything for Peterson, but I reminded myself that he couldn't expect it. I hadn't known he was coming, so how could I have shopped for him? I scanned the gifts he'd brought from L.A. and was relieved that I didn't spot my name on any of them, either.

"I smell dinner." Eli rubbed his hands together.

Andrea popped her head out of the kitchen, grinning. "Come set the table and we'll be ready to eat."

One white tablecloth and my grandparents' wedding china

later, we enjoyed a cozy meal clustered around the kitchen table, making small talk that steered clear of incendiary topics like anything that happened in the last thirty-five years. The kids finished their dinners first and ran in circles around the table while we grown-ups enjoyed our last bites of Andrea's excellent cooking.

Peterson and Eli volunteered for dish duty while I made the whipped cream and Andrea got the kids changed into matching red-and-white striped pajamas. After a round of blueberry pie, made this morning from some of Eli's berries I had stashed in the freezer, we settled in the living room to open gifts.

Andrea chose the recliner so she could guard the presents from J.W. and Izzy's eager little fingers. Even their good manners could only be stretched so far.

Peterson and I exchanged a look before we sat down. For once we agreed on something, wordlessly taking opposite ends of the sofa to put as much distance between us as possible. Eli, oblivious, plopped down between us and slung an arm around my shoulders. I leaned into him, breathing in his familiar scent—laundry soap, fir boughs, spicy aftershave, with a hint of blueberry pie.

I felt the wall I'd put up to guard myself from Peterson start to dissolve. Eli was exactly the buffer I needed to let go of my fears. I could hardly remember what I'd been worried about anyway, now that his arm was around me.

"Are we going to take turns or just dive in?" Andrea asked.

"Let's let the kids go for it, and then we can take turns," I suggested. "They have a lot to unwrap."

Andrea chuckled and swiftly sorted the presents into two piles for the twins, who sat eagerly on the floor, bouncing in place with excitement as she lined up the gifts so they'd unwrap the same ones at the same time.

On Andrea's word, they ripped into their first two packages—the gifts I'd chosen. I hoped they liked what I'd gotten them—miniature barns filled with farm animals. I hoped they'd remember their visits to Nana's house when they played with them at home. Squeals erupted as they uncovered the toys.

A success. They admired them briefly and then tore into the next boxes. The plaid paper said they were from Eli. Inside, two real sheriff's badges and two toy police cars were received gleefully. The kids zoomed the cars around on the floor and crashed them into each other, and Izzy quickly discovered that the cars would erupt in noisy sirens if you pushed on the roof.

"Sorry," Eli said sheepishly to Andrea, who just laughed.

"Hopefully they'll wear the batteries out before we get home," she joked.

Peterson's gifts were predictably over the top. A pair of cashmere teddy bears, a porcelain tea set for Izzy, a beautifully handmade bow-and-arrow set for J.W. They hugged the teddy bears briefly and then stared at the other two gifts, their expressions dismayed. Then, after some kind of magical silent twin communication, they swapped boxes.

I leaned forward slightly to gage Peterson's reaction, bracing myself for his flood of displeasure at seeing the twins reject what he'd chosen for them. But he just laughed and accepted the tiny cup of imaginary tea that J.W. shyly offered to him. The last shred of fear I'd been hanging onto melted away, and I snuggled back into the sofa to watch the kids open their remaining presents, the ones from their parents.

I watched Andrea's face, too. I saw her delight as she shared her children's enjoyment and also a tiny smidge of regret that Steve wasn't there to witness it, too. When the kids had finally opened everything in their piles and began playing with their new toys in earnest, it was our turn.

Chapter 13

Andrea distributed the gifts from her and Steven, with an apology to Eli that she didn't have anything for him as she handed packages to her dad and me.

Eli patted his stomach. "No worries. That dinner was a gift to beat all gifts."

She'd gotten me and Peterson matching Fair Isle sweaters. "I picked them up when we took the kids to Scotland this summer," she explained when we opened the paper. I tugged mine on over my head. Peterson seemed to debate a moment, and then did the same.

Peterson's presents were next. A beautiful emerald bracelet for Andrea, a bottle of 15-year-old Scotch for Eli that he'd picked up at the liquor store this morning. Then, to my surprise, he pulled a small package from his pocket and handed it to me. Unlike the others, it was not perfectly wrapped in shiny paper with matching ribbons and bows on it. It was clumsily covered in what looked like a decorated brown paper grocery bag, with too much tape and a piece of yarn binding it all together.

"The kids helped me wrap it," he explained.

"It's beautiful. Thank you." I smiled at the twins as I accepted the gift. He was smart to recruit their help; if it'd been from him alone, I wouldn't have taken it so eagerly. He had a poor history of choosing gifts for me. Usually they revolved around some form of physical self-improvement: a gym membership, a gift certificate for liposuction, a chemical peel at a medical spa. Stuff *he* thought I needed, but I didn't particularly want.

With some trepidation, I pulled the paper off the small box and opened it. A key rested inside. More specifically, it was a car key, the jellybean-shaped electronic kind. It bore the distinctive, shield-shaped Porsche logo.

I looked up at him. "What is this?"

"Don't say no, Leona. I want you to have it," he said quickly.

"A key?" I asked stupidly.

"I ordered you a new car. That's why I've been on my phone so much the last couple days; I was negotiating with the dealership in Bend. They can't deliver it until tomorrow, but I had them FedEx the key so you had something to unwrap. It's white; I hope that's OK..." He trailed off, knitting his eyebrows worriedly at my stunned expression. "This is the present I should have given you decades ago. You were right, earlier, when you said I didn't get to know you, not really. In some ways I can see you better now than I ever did when we were married."

"This doesn't mean we're getting back togeth—" I started, but he cut me off.

"No, no. I miss you, but it's pretty clear we aren't compatible. This is a peace offering, Leona. An apology for everything I put you through."

I blinked back the moisture that rushed to my eyes as I stared at the key in the tiny white box.

Eli nudged me. "Say thanks," he hissed, grinning. "I want to drive it."

"It's the GTS," Peterson added.

That clinched it for me. I couldn't pass up a GTS, not when it was accompanied by a genuine apology. "I don't know what to say except thank you." I bit my lip as guilt twisted in my stomach. "I didn't get you anything, though. I'm sorry, I didn't know—"

Peterson interrupted me again, which would have been annoying under any other circumstances. "You got me this." He gestured around the room. "You got me my family back, Leona. There's no better gift than that. It's something money can't buy."

I swallowed hard and Eli, sensing my swell of emotion, squeezed me close.

"Next round!" Andrea announced, handing me a flat, plaid package.

Beside me, Eli stiffened. "Maybe you should save that one until the real Christmas," he said, swiping it out of my hands. I understood why—a brand-new Porsche was a hard act to follow. But I wanted him to know that the price tag didn't matter. I valued his gift, whatever it was, just as much.

"Don't be silly," I said, swiping it back and tearing into the paper. "I'm sure I'll—" I froze when I saw what the strip of torn giftwrap had exposed. A pair of tanned, toned abs.

"What is that?" Andrea got up and came to look over my shoulder. She leaned down, squinting, and tugged the paper open a little further before I could stop her. "Is that *you*?" she asked Eli.

Eli pulled the rest of the paper off the gift, blushing, revealing the gift. It was a calendar titled *Honeytree Heroes*, and Andrea was right—Eli was the cover model. Shirtless in his sheriff's hat, he posed in the middle of the highway, straddling the yellow line with an adorable German Shepherd puppy tucked under his arm.

"I'm Mr. January," he said sheepishly, flipping it to the back and pointing to the thumbnail of the first month. "The rest is other people."

I scanned the tiny images of the rest of the year. A volunteer firefighter, biceps flexed, with a pair of Dalmatians. A rear view of a paramedic with a cat perched on his shoulder. A Forest Service search-and-rescue officer, mounted on a horse and wearing a very tiny pair of shorts. Now it was my turn to blush.

"It benefits the county animal shelter," Eli explained, his cheeks still flaming as he avoided eye contact with Peterson.

"Um..." I flipped the calendar to January and soaked in the larger view. "Is it OK if I keep it on this month all year?"

"You like it?" he asked.

"I love it," I said definitively. I set it to the side and pulled out the last remaining gifts from under the tree. I handed one each to Andrea and Eli. "Your turn."

They opened them simultaneously. I'd made a gift basket for each of them, tucked full of little treats I'd collected throughout the year that I thought they'd like. Oregonian wines and homemade blueberry jam for Andrea and Steve, inside jokes for Eli like a Costco-sized pack of Doublemint gum, his favorite. They both got a good chuckle out of it.

"Uh oh," Andrea said, noticing Izzy's yawn. "Time for some people to hit the hay so Santa can come down the chimney."

"I guess that's my cue, too," Eli said. After bidding good night to the twins as Andrea led them upstairs, he pushed himself up from the couch. "Can I talk to you a minute before I go, Leona?"

I nodded, worried by the seriousness of his expression after such a nice evening. I hoped he still wasn't on his whole "give your ex a chance" kick just because of the unfortunate mistletoe zone mishap and Peterson's crazy gifts. We grabbed our jackets and I followed him out to the porch and then the driveway, just outside the circle of the cottage's glow. The dark winter night had a piercing chill that turned our breath into clouds, but the sky was crystal-clear. A swath of brilliant stars stretched across the inky sky like a flurry of snowflakes.

"What's up?" I asked him, dreading the answer.

"I didn't want to ruin the evening, but I have some bad news. Here, I made a copy." He pulled a piece of paper out of his jacket pocket and passed it to me. I squinted at it in the dim light, unable to make out anything except the words at the top that told me it was from the medical examiner's office.

"Homer's report?" I guessed.

Eli nodded. "It doesn't look good for Peterson, unfortunately. I think he's going to have to stay in town a while longer."

My breath caught. "Why? Did they change the cause of death back to blunt force?"

Eli shook his head. "Worse. Homer was poisoned by injection. Someone stuck him full of antifreeze. That, combined with his blood alcohol content, did him in."

I felt sick to my stomach. It wasn't a freak accident or a health issue; someone really had intended to kill Homer. "How awful! I don't understand why's that bad for Peterson, though."

"He's a doctor, Leona. Plus, he's from out of town, and he was the last one to see Homer alive, and they didn't exactly have a friendly exchange. As soon as it gets out that Homer was killed by injection, lots of fingers are going to be pointed his direction."

"He wouldn't do that," I protested. "He's a jerk sometimes, but he's a good doctor. He takes the Hippocratic oath seriously.

'First, do no harm.' He wouldn't use his medical knowledge to *hurt* someone, not on purpose."

"I believe it, but until I can prove otherwise, he has to stick around. Can you convince him to stay another day?"

I sighed. As warm as I was feeling toward Peterson—helped a great deal by my new Porsche—I knew our truce was fragile. It'd be a whole lot easier to stay cordial if I didn't have to see him every day. "Can't you break the bad news? You guys have the whole buddy-buddy thing going on. I think he'll take it better coming from you."

Eli shook his head. "I don't want him to know what's going on—at least, not until I dig around a little bit. If I come out and tell him that he's moved back to the top of the suspect list, he might run back home and lawyer up. If anything is going to arouse the DA's suspicion, it's the prime suspect hiring a big city defense attorney. Let me quietly clear things up, and he can be on his way, none the wiser."

"You want me to lie to him?" I frowned. It wasn't like Eli to ask me to do something like that.

"No—just don't tell him about the report. Make up some excuse for him to stay another day." Eli rubbed his chin and looked past me at Peterson's gold Rolls parked next to my Suburban. I must have looked skeptical, because then he added, "Do you trust me?"

I nodded immediately. If there was one thing I knew, it was that Eli never let me down.

"Then will you try, at least? If he refuses to stay another day, then you can show him the report, send him home to my guest room, and I'll convince him it's in his interest—one way or another."

"I'll see what I can do. But promise me that first thing in the morning, you'll get that security camera footage from Ed so you can see that Peterson was telling the truth. He may have scuffled with Homer, but he didn't hurt him seriously. Then you can cross him off the list and find the real killer."

"I promise." He planted a kiss on my cheek and strode off into the dark beyond the chicken coop. I heard the click of the gate latch between our properties and then the quiet crinkle of his footsteps in the grass between the blueberry bushes faded.

Well, I couldn't stand here all night in the driveway. I went inside to do Eli's dirty work.

Peterson was surprisingly easy to convince. Maybe it was the afterglow of the meal and gift exchange, but with the thin excuse of attending the Walk-Thru Nativity the next day, he quickly agreed to stay one more day. I felt a little guilt at repaying his generosity with a big fat lie, but I trusted Eli, and Eli said it was in Peterson's best interest.

After Peterson left for Eli's, yawning, still wearing the sweater that matched mine, Andrea and I filled the kids' stockings over a half-glass of wine each.

"It means a lot to me that you accepted Dad's apology," Andrea said, apropos of nothing. "It gives me hope. I was worried that Steve and I might end up the same way."

"What way?" I tucked a chocolate orange covered in bright foil on top of J.W.'s stocking and turned to her.

"I don't know—angry? Alienated? The twins are so little, and if we split up, I don't want there to be animosity between us. I want us to be able to celebrate Christmas together without causing them pain." Her last word nearly silent, like the idea had stolen her breath.

"You're not going to split up." I guided her over to the sofa, the stockings having been stuffed to the limits.

Andrea's face was flat and strained as she finished off her glass of wine. "You don't know that. Nobody can know that. You and Dad had thirty good years together before it all fell apart. Even if Steven and I make it another year or two, how can we possibly do this for our whole lives? We're already in counseling!"

"I know it because you're already working on it. You're already recognizing and addressing the issues. That's how you fix them! I wish your dad and I had done that instead of just pushing it all down and letting it build up for decades. They weren't good years. Honestly, they were all kind of cruddy."

"Don't say that. I had a great childhood," Andrea said stoutly.

I smoothed her hair where a flat-ironed lock had sprung back into a spiral curl that matched my own. "I'm glad. That's why we stuck it out for as long as we did, and I don't regret a minute of it."

"No?"

"No."

Chapter 14

December 24

B*eep, beep, beep.* The sound from the driveway woke me. I cracked open my eyes, moaning slightly at the stiff neck I'd been bequeathed by the somewhat lumpy couch cushions underneath my head. Oh well, small price to pay for a house full of grandbabies.

It was still dark out, but the clock claimed it was morning, so I yawned and trudged to the kitchen to see what all the beeping was about. In the early morning dim, I saw the glowing taillights of a flatbed truck backing up to the house.

Beep, beep, beep.

Perched on the back of it was a white-as-snow, pretty-as-a-dove, brand-spanking-new 718 GTS with a huge red bow tied to the front. Magical. It felt like Santa just might be real. I tugged my jacket on over my PJs and ran out in my bare feet. I regretted it the minute my soles hit the gravel.

"Ouch, ouch, ouch," I said in time with the backup beeps as I picked my way gingerly toward the cab of the truck.

"Morning!" The passenger in the truck, a young guy with spiky short dreads and a Bend Porsche dealership patch sewn on his shirt pocket, swung out and checked his clip board. "You Leona Davis?"

I nodded, and he passed me the clipboard to sign. It felt like he was handing me one of those big lottery checks. I signed it in a daze as he and the driver collaborated to lower a ramp from the tailgate, then backed my new car down it so it blocked in the other three cars parked there—Andrea's rental sedan, my ancient Suburban, and Peterson's Rolls. The two men circled the car, carefully inspecting it to make sure it hadn't incurred any damage during the delivery.

Then the driver got back in the truck and the other delivery guy returned to shake my hand and retrieve his clipboard. He tore off a sheet and handed it to me along with a fat envelope of information about the car. "You're good to go, ma'am. Congrats on the new ride. Merry Christmas!"

Still in a daze, I waved goodbye and watched them head down the driveway. It wasn't until they'd turned onto the highway toward the freeway that I shook myself out of my trance and went to admire the car myself.

It was like a dream. Even sitting in my poky little farmyard, surrounded by a motley crew of other vehicles like we were in the middle of a used car lot, the new GTS looked like it was the star of a magazine spread. It was immaculate.

I couldn't believe it was mine—or that it came without strings attached. Behind me, someone cleared their throat, startling me. I jumped and whirled around. It was just Peterson, holding up his phone, his face apologetic.

"I walked over when I got the delivery notification," he said. "Nice PJs. Where are your shoes?"

"I didn't have time to dress for success," I said a little sourly, but with the car in my view, I couldn't be crabby for long. "This was too much, you know. I shouldn't accept it."

"You have to. If it helps, remember that you got the short end of the stick with the prenup. You never should have signed it to begin with, frankly."

I gave him a crooked smile. I'd signed it in good faith, never expecting that our relationship would go south, but I guess nobody does. I shrugged. "I loved you."

"I loved you, too. That's why I should have been more generous from the get-go. I hope this makes up for it a little. Plus, my business has doubled since our TV appearance went viral, so I can afford it."

Motherclucker. He made money off the worst moment of my life. Any guilt I felt over not getting him a Christmas present evaporated in an instant. I smacked his arm with the back of my hand. "In that case, I think you owe me a new car every Christmas."

#

I left Peterson and Andrea basking in the glow of the twins' glee as they emptied their stockings out on the living room rug and pawed through the contents, while I ran to town to pick up the promised doughnuts from Ed. I pulled the Suburban up to the back of the tiny brick building and knocked at the rear entrance. The smell of cinnamon-sugar wafted from the vent to the right of the door, making my mouth water.

Ed answered, wiping his hands on the apron tied around his waist. "I need to fry another batch still. Do you mind waiting a few? I can pour you a cup of joe if you want to come on in. I'm closed for the holidays, so it's quiet."

"I won't turn down a hot cup of coffee on a cold morning." I wouldn't turn down one of those doughnuts, either. I followed him into the diner's small kitchen area. A counter separated it from the tables, but the seating was all empty, save one person at a counter stool—Eli, in full uniform, with an electronic tablet in his hand. He flipped it around so I could see that it was Ed's security monitor. It had a video all queued up.

"Want to watch it with me?"

My curiosity piqued, I slid onto the stool next to Eli, gratefully accepting the white mug of coffee that Ed pushed across the counter toward me.

"Don't judge me too harshly when you see what's on there," Ed said, turning back to his fryer. In a deft motion, he slipped some raw dough from a tray into the bubbling oil. "I had my reasons."

I was right—Ed *had* been hiding something on the footage. I exchanged a look with Eli. My look said *I told you* and his said *don't be smug*. I reached over and hit the "Play" arrow on the monitor.

A view from the Greasy Spoon's back lot came to life. Though most of the monitor was filled with the parking area, dumpster, and back porch, a triangular sliver in the top right corner of the screen showed the highway and the single pump and front door of Wilds Gas and Go. As the video played, a few lazy cars straggled by on the highway. Eli scrubbed the video ahead until Peterson's flamboyant Rolls Royce pulled into the gas station and parked next to the pump.

I held my breath as I watched the silent exchange. It unfolded much as Peterson had described. Homer started to pump his gas, stumbled into the side of the car, and then Peterson nearly leaped from the driver's seat, gesturing wildly. The figures were too small to make out their expressions, but Peterson suddenly stepped back as Homer threw the first punch. A second one caught him by surprise, knocking him to the side.

"That must be the black eye," Eli commented.

Homer staggered, knocking against the pump and pylons, just as Peterson said it happened. When he came in for another round, Peterson pushed him away—hard. Homer fell flat on the pavement, knocking his head on the concrete.

In the video, Peterson froze. He looked back over his shoulder at the highway and, seeing no one, grabbed Homer under the arms and dragged him into the office, flipping the sign in the window to "Closed" behind him.

My throat tightened. He'd left this part out of his story completely.

Eli paused the video. "This doesn't look good for Peterson," he said, his voice low. "Actually, it looks downright bad."

"Keep going," I urged. "Maybe it gets better."

He started the video, and I gripped my mug tightly, willing the screen to show Homer walking out the door, laughing and talking with Peterson. But only Peterson reappeared. With another furtive look around, he opened his trunk and pulled out his medical kit. I groaned, and Eli hit pause again.

"Did I say bad? I meant really bad."

"Come on, just play the rest of it." I couldn't take any more delays. I had to know what really happened. Eli nodded, and we leaned together to watch Peterson disappear back inside the gas station. I held my breath as minutes passed. Finally Eli scrubbed ten minutes ahead to when Peterson reappeared. He walked briskly to the trunk of the Rolls, stowed his medical bag, pumped his own gas, then got into the driver's seat and drove off down the highway.

Eli stopped the video again and just looked at me.

"I don't think he even has syringes in that bag," I said, feeling inexplicably guilty even though Peterson was the one caught in a lie. "It's regular first aid stuff, plus a stethoscope and BP cuff, if I remember right."

"Why didn't he just tell me he administered first aid, then?" Eli asked. "Why did he lie if he didn't do anything wrong?"

I shook my head. I wish I knew. But nobody knew what happened inside that office except Peterson and Homer—if Homer ever woke up, that is. I shivered, a chill running down my spine despite the hot coffee I still clutched in my hands. "Wait, Peterson wouldn't leave someone who was unconscious. He would have called an ambulance if Homer didn't wake up. Keep going—I bet we'll see Homer come out the front door in just a minute. And then maybe we'll see who *actually* killed him."

Eli nodded gravely. "I hope you're right." He let the video play on as, on the other side of the counter, Ed tended his batch of doughnuts, flipping them in the grease so the browned side was revealed.

For a long stretch there was no action save a hopeful starling in the diner's parking lot. Finally, a car pulled into the gas station and waited at the pump. I held my breath a long minute until it drove off again, having apparently given up on filling their gas tank. Eli scrubbed the video forward until there was more action on the screen.

A pedestrian cut across the gas station's parking lot, heading toward the door. I squinted at the screen. The tiny figure was an oddly dressed man with wild, curly hair. He wore a short green tunic and green-and-white striped tights. *An elf?*

"Is that Rusty Chapman?" I mused aloud.

"I think so."

We watched as Rusty reached the door and paused for a second, staring at the "Closed" sign. Then he pulled the door open and went inside. I drew in my breath.

"What is it?" Eli asked.

"Ruth mentioned that he had a job interview lined up at the gas station. She asked him how it went while we were wrapping gifts with the Knitwits. He said he didn't have the interview, though. He seemed a little upset about it."

Eli frowned, his eyes still trained on the monitor. "Did he say he didn't go or that he didn't have an interview?"

I racked my brain for Rusty's exact wording. "I think he said, 'It didn't happen.' So I guess he had an interview. I assumed it was canceled, but it looks like he showed up for it."

"Let's see how long he's in there." Eli moved the video ahead until the door re-opened, pausing to check the time stamp. "Five minutes. Not long enough for an interview."

"He has something," I said, pointing at a blurred rectangular shape that Rusty clutched in his hands. "What is that?"

Eli let the video play so we could get a better look. "A paper bag, maybe? Could be the money from the till. Maybe Homer told him the interview was off, Rusty got angry and killed him, grabbed the money on the way out."

I bit my lip. I didn't want to believe Rusty was capable of something like that, but I also knew that money was very tight for him. He was eager to get back on his feet now that he had served his prison sentence, and he would have been frustrated to miss out on a potential job, even a low-wage one like gas station attendant. And he might have learned some new skills in prison.

"Or maybe he just bought some beef jerky from a very alive Homer Wilds," I said defensively, pushing back against my own suspicions. "I bet if you keep that video rolling, we'll see Homer walk out that door. Then we'll feel silly we ever thought Rusty could be involved."

Eli looked doubtful, but he let the video play, speeding through sections with little or no action. A white van with a logo on the door pulled around to the back of the gas station. Eli rewound, paused, and zoomed in to read the circular logo. The words were too blurry, but I recognized the image in the center, a ball of yarn with two needles stuck through it like a warm, fuzzy skull-and-crossbones.

"It's the Knitty Gritty van. I bet it was Joan. You know, she had a lot of opinions about Homer's drinking. She was really upset that Ruth asked him to play Santa."

Eli chuckled. "If it was crazy to point fingers at Rusty, it's even crazier to point them at Joan. She's a sweet old lady who knits for charity and volunteers to give Christmas gifts to needy children."

I rolled my eyes. "I'm not saying she killed Homer. I'm saying there are at least two people who might have seen him alive after Peterson left the gas station. We just need to talk to them. If either one is willing to go on record that Homer was alive, then Peterson is off the hook."

Rather than responding, Eli let the video play. A few short minutes after the van pulled behind the building, it drove out the other side. He moved the video forward again, until another pedestrian figure appeared. This time, the person was instantly recognizable—on the screen, Ed exited the back door of the diner, hefting a propane tank in one hand. He walked swiftly across the parking lot, barely pausing to check for cars as he crossed the highway and went straight to the gas station's door.

He knocked at the window and then put his hand to the glass to look inside. I held my breath, unable to keep my eyes off the real Ed on the other side of the counter, who was now removing the golden-brown doughnuts from the fryer to roll in a tray of cinnamon-sugar. The smell was tantalizing.

My attention was drawn back to the screen by Ed's movements. When he didn't receive an answer to a second knock at Wilds Gas and Go, he hauled the propane tank over to the large, cylindrical tank on the side of the building, filled it up, and carried it back over to the back door of the restaurant.

Eli paused the video again and raised his head to look at Ed. Ed turned to move the doughnuts into a box and noticed Eli's expression.

He wiped his hands on his apron and sighed. "You saw it. I know, I should have paid for the propane, but he didn't answer—and I figured he owed me for the trash cleanup anyway."

"Was he the one getting into your dumpster?" I asked.

Ed clicked his tongue. "Yup. First night I put the camera up, I saw him digging in the trash, throwing things around. He took the recyclables to turn in for the bottle deposit and left everything else strewn around the parking lot like a dang raccoon. I told him to knock it off, but of course all I got in return was a string of curse words."

"Is this why you wouldn't let me see the footage before?" Eli asked. "You didn't want to get caught stealing propane?"

Ed nodded guiltily. "Figured it didn't matter unless Homer really was murdered. Then I'd take my lumps. But if he bit the dust on his own, then the free propane just evened our score."

"I see." Eli's attention was back on the monitor. "Did you happen to see him inside the station when you looked through the glass?"

"Nope." Ed moved the box of doughnuts to the top of a stack that was waiting by the back door. "You're good to go with these, Leona. Merry Christmas."

"Thanks so much, Ed. I'll make sure that Ruth gets you a donation receipt." I slid off my stool, but Eli caught the sleeve of my jacket.

"Don't you want to see what happens?" he asked. Curiosity got the better of me, and I leaned over his shoulder to watch the rest.

A couple of cars came and went, the drivers waiting only a few minutes at the pump before driving off again. Eli pushed the video further forward until a dark SUV pulled up to the front door. A tall, broad-shouldered figure exited the driver's side door, and Eli hit pause.

"That's me." He sighed, disappointed, then scrubbed forward so I could see what happened after that in eight-times speed. On the screen, Eli went inside the gas station and came back out right away. A fire truck and ambulance arrived, and paramedics swarmed inside. Then more sheriff's deputies arrived, the gas station was cordoned off, and a coroner's van came. He stopped the video. "That's all she wrote. You know what this means, Leona." I didn't like how serious his expression was as he studied my face.

"What?"

"Peterson has some explaining to do. What's in that medical kit, for starters. And why he lied about it. I'm going to head over to your house and have a chat with him. Ideally, we can clear this all up in a few minutes. You want to come?"

I nodded, my heart heavy. "Do me a favor, will you? Wait until I get there to start questioning him? I have a bunch of doughnuts to load up first."

113

Chapter 15

I found Eli and Peterson on their hands and knees on the kitchen floor when I got home, racing the toy police cars that belonged to J.W. and Izzy. The twins, who presumably had put them up to it, had lost interest and wandered off to play with their other gifts, but the two grown men were still crouched on the worn linoleum near the table, trash-talking each other.

"You're going down, Pete. You're going to lose so bad, California's going to revoke your driver's license." Eli narrowed his eyes as Peterson counted them down.

"Three, two, one, *go!*"

They shoved their cars toward the fridge at the same time, looking up in surprise when I put my foot out, sending both cars veering off course. Eli's crashed into the bottom of the cabinets and Peterson's disappeared out the kitchen door into the entryway. A faint rattle told me it'd found the umbrella stand.

Eli scrambled to his feet and helped Peterson up, then dusted off the knees of his uniform.

I pursed my lips. "My kitchen floor is clean, thank you very much. Can we just get this over with? I'd like it if we could all move on with our day. I have doughnuts to deliver."

Peterson gave me a quizzical look. "Get what over with?"

Eli sighed. "Sorry about this, Pete. But I need to ask you a few more questions about what happened at the gas station. I got a chance to look at the security camera footage, and what's on tape doesn't exactly match your story."

Peterson's whole body stilled, the residual playfulness from his earlier game evaporating. He pulled out a chair from the table and sat down in it, his eyes unfocused. "I had a feeling this might come up."

Eli sat beside him. "Why'd you leave so much out of your story? If you've got a good explanation, I'm all ears."

Peterson looked up at me pleadingly. "You know me better than anyone. Love me or hate me, you don't think I hurt him, do you?"

"No, of course not. But I do think you owe Eli an explanation for why you lied."

"We know the first part of your story was true," Eli said, his voice rumbling low. "But then you pushed Homer pretty hard. He fell and hit his head. Tell me about what happened after that."

Peterson sighed. "I was worried he might have a head injury, so I dragged him inside to put some ice on it." He gnawed the inside of his cheek pensively. "He woke up pretty groggy. I grabbed my med kit from the trunk—you know I always have it with me," he added to me.

I nodded, and he continued. "I checked his pupils, then took his BP. His reflexes were poor, but I chalked that up to the alcohol. I told him to keep the ice pack on his head and call an ambulance if he had any coordination problems. Then I left."

Eli sat back in his chair. "I don't believe you."

"That's everything I remember," Peterson said simply.

I understood Eli's skepticism. If Peterson was telling the truth now, then why did he leave out the part about helping Homer when he gave his first statement? I couldn't make sense of it, especially now that I knew for sure that Rusty had seen Homer alive after Peterson left.

"Why didn't you just say that before?" I asked.

Peterson grimaced. "When I heard he died, I thought maybe it was due to a head injury that I missed. Since I technically treated and released him, I worried I could be sued for malpractice. Selfish of me, I guess. I probably should have taken him to a hospital myself, just in case. Then he'd probably still be alive."

His expression was so anguished, I couldn't help feeling sorry for him. I walked around the table and put my hand on his shoulder, squeezing it comfortingly.

Eli didn't seem as convinced. "If you don't mind, I need to see the contents of that bag," he said.

"It's out in the trunk." Peterson patted my hand and then scooted his chair back. We walked outside together, and Eli produced the keys he'd confiscated, popping the trunk of the Rolls. Peterson pulled out the leather medical bag and showed Eli which key on the ring fit the bag's brass lock. "What are you looking for, if you don't mind me asking?"

Eli took the bag from him and unlocked it. "Turns out that Homer was killed with an injection of antifreeze. The antifreeze itself was probably from Homer's shop, but I need to know whether you have any sharps in this kit."

Peterson paled, gripping the edge of the open trunk to steady himself. His reaction surprised me. I'd seen the kit before, and I couldn't remember any needles in it. Maybe he was just rattled by the method of murder that Eli had described. I'd spent so much time hanging around Eli and chatting about his cases that I forgot what it was like, being shocked by crime.

Eli took the bag to the porch and carefully laid out the contents, one item at a time, on the clean surface of the table between the Adirondack chairs.

A stethoscope. A blood pressure cuff. A thermometer, a pulse oximeter. A plastic box full of bandages and antiseptic and Tylenol packets. Face masks, hand sanitizer, alcohol wipes, cotton swaps wrapped in sterile packaging.

I yawned and began to turn away.

"Wait!" Eli's voice came sharply as he pulled the last item out of the bag. He held up a small, black zippered case. Peterson passed his hand over his face as though he couldn't bear to look, cringing away from Eli.

With a look of trepidation, Eli unzipped the case, laying it open on the small table between the Adirondack chairs. A row of individually wrapped syringes, one large and several smaller, greeted my eyes, along with a small glass vial with a printed label.

"What is this?" Eli demanded. Peterson mumbled something I couldn't make out, his eyes on the porch floor, and apparently Eli couldn't understand him any better than I could, because he asked, "What?"

"Botox!" Peterson burst out. "It's Botox, OK? It was for Leona, for Christmas."

I blinked, speechless. He was blaming his bag of murder needles on *my wrinkles*?

Motherclucker.

"Well, obviously, I didn't give it to you!" he rushed to add when he noticed my expression. "Don't be mad—I really thought you'd like it. I asked the ladies at my office and they said they'd be thrilled to get free Botox. But once I got here, I realized it was a bad idea, and I ordered you the Porsche instead."

"Thank goodness, or else you might have been the one who got murdered," I muttered under my breath.

Andrea stuck her head out the door and frowned at us. "Aren't you all freezing out here?"

I realized I'd left my jacket inside, and goosebumps were raised on both my arms. I rubbed them away. "We'll be right in."

"You'll be right in. Pete and I need to take a ride down to my office," Eli said grimly. He zipped up the case and began packing everything back into the medical bag. "He has a few things to clear up."

Andrea stepped out onto the porch, closing the door behind her. "Is he under arrest?" she asked. Her voice had a hard edge.

"No. But he needs—" Eli began, but Andrea cut him off, her eyes flashing.

"Then he's not going anywhere with you. If you have anything to say to Mr. Davis, you can say it to me, his lawyer. Otherwise, back off." She jabbed her finger at him, cutting a formidable figure. Eli raised his hands defensively and took a step back.

I'd forgotten what it was like, seeing her in action; she'd taken time off from her career as a criminal defense attorney to raise J.W. and Izzy. But now her switch had flipped. Gone was the sweet, soft, stay-at-home mom with perfectionist tendencies. Now, she was a pit bull defending her client. And she turned her fierce gaze on me next.

"I can't believe you're letting him do this to Dad. You know very well he didn't kill anyone. He has no criminal record, he has no violent tendencies, he has no motive to rob a backwoods convenience store for a few hundo in cash." Andrea ticked off the counterevidence on her fingers.

"Thanks, Anda-panda," Peterson said, grabbing her hand. "You mean well, but Eli does, too. I think I know him well enough to say that he'll be fair."

I nodded. "He will. Eli's just following the evidence, and that means that he now needs to talk to the *other* people who may have seen Homer alive, right?" I turned to Eli, begging him with my eyes. While I wasn't too pleased with Peterson, I hoped Eli wouldn't jump to any conclusions, either.

Before Andrea's dreams of a happy family holiday were crushed, I wanted to be one hundred percent sure that Peterson had been involved in the crime. And while I had a strong suspicion he'd "disappeared" a chicken, it stretched belief that he'd murder a gas station attendant over a little scratched paint. Even he wasn't that superficial or vindictive.

Eli pressed his lips together, looking torn. "I want to believe you, I really do, but—"

"You have his car keys. You have his medical kit. It's not like he can go anywhere. Let us have Christmas. Twenty-four more hours."

Between my begging and Andrea's stubborn stare, Eli didn't have a chance. "Fine. I'll give it a day. If Rusty or Joan can confirm they saw Homer alive, then great. But if not, I won't have a choice, Pete. I'll have to—"

"I know," Peterson interrupted. "I understand."

Chapter 16

Still unsettled, I drove the now-cooled doughnuts back to the Church of the Everlasting, where the Walk-Thru Nativity would be set up in their hilltop parking lot. On the way, I picked up the cheesecakes from Sara at the Rx Café. When I pulled up to the church, Ruth's car was already parked on the street.

I located her in the church basement, where she was setting up the refreshments tables in front of the church's pink, Fifties-era kitchen. Her hair was bundled up into a huge bun—her "getting things done" hairdo—and she was hustling like her life depended on it.

She lit up when she saw the cheesecakes in my arms and motioned to the fridge behind her. "Put 'em there. Can you give me a hand spreading out the tablecloths?"

"Sure." I slid the dessert boxes into the fridge and went to grab the other end of the banquet-length tablecloth Ruth had unfolded. "I've got a cluckload of doughnuts and cider in the back of my car, too. The Pastry Palace said they'd deliver the pies later."

"Fantastic. Phew. I think we might actually pull this off." Ruth straightened the tablecloth, plopped a wreath in the center of it, and stood back to admire the effect. Seemingly pleased with her artistic touch, she then moved on to the next table.

I followed her, obediently repeating the motions to spread out the huge tablecloth. This table got an angel centerpiece. The third table had a couple of star-shaped candleholders, and the fourth one was reserved for the cash box and some glittery pinecones. When we were finished putting out the crock pots and cups for the hot cider, she dusted her hands and grinned mischievously at me. "Now how about those doughnuts? Think anyone will miss a few?"

She helped me carry the boxes from my car down the precarious basement stairs and, despite her earlier threats, didn't actually eat any of them, though she did open a box to breathe in the sweet, spicy scent. Her stomach growled audibly, and she snapped the box closed. "I better put these away before I get myself in trouble," she grinned. "Want to grab some lunch?"

I grimaced. "I don't think anywhere in town is open on Christmas Eve. I probably should get back to the farm, anyway."

"Oh, right, you have company." Ruth giggled. "How's it going with that ex of yours? He seems—well, a little weird. I can't picture you two together at all."

I nodded. "I know. I can't, either. It's going OK, though. I just have to convince Eli that he's not a killer."

Ruth's big blue eyes nearly popped out of her skull. "Wait, Eli thinks Peterson killed Homer Wilds?"

"Yep. Well, maybe. For a while, he thought maybe Peterson was the last person to see Homer alive. But get this—the Greasy Spoon has a new security camera. Eli and I saw some footage from the day Homer died, and Peterson's story doesn't match what's on the camera. Plus, Homer was killed by injection, and Peterson had syringes in his car."

"Whoa. Do you think he did it?"

I shook my head. "He might be a jerk sometimes, but I know him. He wouldn't do that. I think it'll work out OK once Eli does a little more digging. On the security footage, a couple other people stopped by the gas station after Peterson left. If one of those people saw Homer alive, then Peterson won't be in trouble."

"You mean, maybe one of them did it instead?" Ruth raised an eyebrow, and I nodded. "Who else was there?"

"Joan came by in her yarn store van and parked behind the building for a few minutes. I thought that was kind of weird."

Ruth shrugged. "It makes sense, actually."

"It does? What would she be doing there, lurking behind the gas station?"

"She was probably picking up Gifting Tree donations to bring over to the community center," Ruth explained. "The gas station is one of the drop-off locations where people can leave toys. It's pretty convenient since everyone stops there for gas anyway."

"Oh."

"Who else was on the tape?" Ruth prodded.

I hesitated slightly. "You're not going to like it. You know how Rusty had a job interview?"

"It was canceled, though," Ruth said swiftly. She looked like she might burst into tears. "Remember? He said it was canceled. He didn't go."

"No, he said 'it didn't happen.' But he went to meet with Homer, Ruth. I saw him walk inside the shop. And I saw him walk out a few minutes later carrying something—Eli thinks it might have been the money from the till," I added apologetically. "Money's tight for him right now, and maybe he got upset about the job falling through..."

Ruth's face crumpled and she took a step back from me, twisting her hands together anxiously. "Rusty wouldn't steal. If he needed money, he'd ask me for it. He can't go back to jail, Leona."

I could sense she was teetering on the edge of panic. "You're right. I'm just hopeful Rusty will swear that Homer was alive and well when he left the gas station so that Peterson can go back to LA, and I can relax in my own home. I've been reminded why marriage is not for me."

Ruth chuckled at my self-deprecating tone, although her forehead was still creased with worry. She located her purple tapestry purse under a pile of grocery sacks in the kitchen and got out her phone, her hands trembling. "I'm going to call him."

She meant Rusty. I sucked the air through my teeth. Though Eli hadn't told me to keep any of the information on the security tape to myself, I had an inkling that he wouldn't like me tipping off potential witnesses—nor potential suspects. "Maybe let the sheriff's department handle it? I'm sure it's nothing. Eli will clear it up with him, I'm sure."

"I'm sorry, Leona. He's my brother." She held the phone to her ear while she waited for Rusty to pick up. A second later, the line connected, and Ruth let loose on him. "I'm pretty ticked off at you, Ruston Darrell Chapman! Why? Because you lied to my face. Yes, you did. Don't deny it. You were on film marching your skinny rear end into Wilds Gas and Go for that interview, and you told me that 'it didn't happen.' Well, it did happen. And you better have a darn good explanation why you told me a tall tale about it."

Ruth listened, bosom heaving after her rant, as Rusty answered. A minute later, she interrupted him. "Hang on. I'm going to put you on speaker so Leona can hear." She hit a button and put her phone on the table. "Go ahead, Rusty. Tell her what you just told me."

Rusty's crackling voice came over the line. "Ugh, Ruthie. I don't like airing my dirty laundry like this. It's bad enough that everyone knows I just got out of the slammer."

"It's OK. I won't tell anyone," I assured him. "Well, except maybe Eli, but he's going to ask you anyway."

Rusty sighed, his voice resigned. "I went to the interview, and the 'Closed' sign was up. Right away I knew it was a bad sign. Probably should have turned around right there, but I went in anyway. Homer heard me come in and called from the back room. When I found him, he looked like a dog's dinner. Said he had a belligerent customer earlier. Didn't feel like interviewing me."

"You should have rescheduled," Ruth objected.

"I suggested that we do it the next day and he said no. Said he'd thought better of hiring a criminal and preferred someone more trustworthy. So I left."

"Why didn't you just say that when I asked you at Knitty Gritty?" Ruth demanded.

"I felt like a loser, I guess. Sorry about that, Ruthie. I should have told you."

"See?" Ruth mouthed across the table to me. I nodded. Rusty's story sounded genuine, and even better, he'd actually spoken with Homer.

"So Homer was alive when you left the gas station?" I asked, just to be sure.

"Yup. Alive and ornery like always."

"One last thing, Rusty. What was in the paper bag, the one you carried out of the shop?" I held my breath as I waited for his answer.

"Coupla Twinkies and a Mountain Dew. My consolation prize. Spent my last two-dollar bill on it—you know how Granddad always gave them to us for our birthdays, Ruth?" Rusty chuckled ruefully. "I'm so broke, I had to bust open my old piggy bank."

Ruth clucked her tongue sympathetically. "We'll find you a job soon, don't worry. In the meantime, if you need money, just come to me, OK?"

"I hate to ask you for anything else." Rusty sounded miserable.

"Hush. Why else do I work so hard if it isn't to help the people I love?" Ruth hung up the phone and shot me a smile. "Well, that's settled. Thanks for humoring me. Will I see you tonight at the Nativity? The grandkids'll love it."

I tilted my head, trying to decide. "Andrea and Peterson are going to bring the twins to see the animals. I think I might just stay home. I haven't had a minute to myself these past few days, and I just want to put my feet up on the porch and watch the chickens. Plus, church isn't really my scene." I gestured wryly to our surroundings.

The décor in the church basement looked like the Brady Bunch went on an Italian vacation. Mismatched furniture in loud tones clashed with classical oil paintings of European landmarks, interspersed with religious iconography. The wood-paneled walls were strung with tinsel garlands, and the baseboards on three sides of the room were lined with fully decorated Christmas trees. It was cozy but chaotic, and I just needed some calm.

She rolled her eyes. "Come on, it's Christmas. That's one of those times that church is everybody's scene. You got married in a church, you'll get buried near a church, and you celebrate

Christmas and Easter in a church, right?"

"I got married in a country club," I objected.

Ruth flashed me a huge, knowing grin. "And how'd that work out for you?"

"Fine," I growled. "I'll see you tonight."

Chapter 17

Eli and Peterson were still racing cars on my kitchen floor with the kids when I got back to the farm. Andrea roped J.W. and Izzy into sitting at the table and fed them lunch while I filled her, Peterson, and Eli in on what Rusty had told me and Ruth in the church basement.

"I told you," Andrea said smugly. She dampened a paper towel with water and wiped a smudge of peanut butter off Izzy's chin, then sent her outside to play with J.W., who was already spinning in circles on the grass by the lilac bushes.

I grinned at her. "Yup. You told us all."

Peterson slumped back into his chair. "Thank goodness. I wasn't looking forward to spending Christmas in jail."

"Happy now?" Andrea asked Eli. "Dad couldn't have killed anyone because the victim was alive after he left. Done and dusted."

Eli nodded slowly. "I think we can rule you out, Pete. I have to say, I'm relieved, too—even though I'm not thrilled with the investigative methods. Now I have twice the paperwork." He shot me a look, which I shrugged off. By now, he should be aware that I don't keep secrets from Ruth, and obviously Ruth wouldn't keep them from her brother. If Eli didn't want me to conduct my own little investigations, then he should keep his evidence to himself.

"Sorry not sorry," I said. He grinned at me, shaking his head.

Peterson chuckled, seemingly recovered from his dismay over everything. "Does this mean I can have my kit back?"

Eli nodded and slid the med kit from under the kitchen table.

"And my car keys?"

Eli pulled them from his pocket and handed them over. "Now I have my afternoon cut out for me. Yay, paperwork," he said, making a face at me.

"I think you mean 'thanks for doing my job for me.' You're welcome. Will we see you tonight, or will you be too busy?" I asked him.

Eli nodded. "I'll be there, but I'm on duty, so I probably won't be able to hang out."

"Guarding the baby Jesus?"

"Yup. And if any camels escape, I'll be wrangling them." He winked at me.

After Eli left for his office, Peterson went to stow his bag back in the trunk of his car, and I took the opportunity to have a private word with Andrea.

"You're glowing," I commented. "I think we may have found the cure for what ails you."

She rolled her eyes. "What're you talking about?"

"You were your dad's lawyer for about fifteen minutes, and it's like it woke up your soul. That's the answer to your unhappiness, sweetheart. You're ready to go back to work!"

"Huh." She leaned to look out the window at J.W. and Izzy. They were joking and playing with Peterson in the driveway, dodging his grasp as he pretended to try and catch them. "Maybe you're right. They're so independent now. It's possible I've been a little bit bored."

I shrugged. "Think about it, anyway. You're an amazing mom, but that doesn't mean you have to stay home. Not everyone's cut out to be a housewife forever."

And didn't I know it.

The kids came back in and begged me to read to them, so I took them to the living room, settling both of them on my lap with a stack of stories. They fell in love with a scented Christmas book with scratch-and-sniff panels, and we must have read it five times. On the sixth time through, Peterson came in just as I scratched the sticker on a pine tree. Izzy leaned forward to inhale the scent, then passed the book to J.W. so he could have a turn.

When J.W. finished, he held the book out for Peterson to sniff, too. "Here, Gamp. It smells like tree smell."

Peterson sniffed it dutifully and shared a grin with me. He waited until we finished the rest of the book and the kids ran off to play before he revealed the real reason he'd come to find me.

"I decided that I'm not going to the church thing with you and Andrea this evening."

I raised an eyebrow. I couldn't blame him for wanting to leave now that he'd been officially exonerated of any wrongdoing in relation to Homer's death. Though he'd been too quick to anger over the damage to his car, he'd only acted in self-defense, and he'd done his best to help Homer after the fact. But I was shocked at my own disappointment that he was leaving.

"The kids will miss you, but I understand why you'd rather blow this popsicle stand," I said. "It'll be nice to get back to civilization, huh?"

Peterson chuckled. "I'm not hitting the road just yet. Truthfully? I kind of hate to leave this place. You've shown me what

I've missed, living my whole life in the big city. That's why I want to do something nice for you tonight, Leona."

"Nicer than a brand-new Porsche?" I grinned at him.

"I want to cook you and Andrea and the grandkids dinner, if that's OK. I don't know if we'll ever spent a holiday all together like this again, and I just want one more family meal together."

Leaving Peterson alone in my house for a couple of hours? A week ago, the idea would have been unimaginable. But now, it didn't sound so terrible.

To my surprise, I actually trusted the guy.

Chapter 18

The neighborhood around the Church of the Everlasting was packed with cars. Andrea's eyes widened as she wound the rental car through the side streets, looking for a spot.

"The church parking lot's blocked off for the Nativity, otherwise we could park closer," I explained.

"I had no idea that so many people even lived in Honeytree!"

"They don't. I think most people live out in the sticks, like I do. But everyone shows up for these community events."

Andrea finally found a spot a few blocks away, and the kids piled out of their booster seats onto the sidewalk. We joined the many families straggling toward the church parking lot. Izzy bobbed beside me, skipping and squeezing my hand every so often. J.W. clung to Andrea's arm, a little more cautious about what lay ahead of us.

A temporary fence had been constructed around the entire lot to block our view of the Nativity itself, which only added to Izzy's excitement.

"What's inside, Nana?" she asked. "Is there candy?"

"Nope, but there are doughnuts."

J.W., who'd been hanging back slightly, suddenly bounced ahead. "Doughnuts?!"

We finally reached the arch that marked the entrance, but the gates were closed. The only part of the Nativity that was visible was a glowing star hung high above the center of the maze.

Cal Goodbody, the charismatic pastor who led the Church of the Everlasting, was stationed in front of the doors. I hardly recognized him without his usual natty suit-and-tie. Instead, he wore a long white robe and a crown of gold plastic leaves circling his head. When a few more family groups had joined ours, he pretended to read from the Styrofoam "tablet" he carried, his voice ringing out majestically.

"I am Caesar Augustus. I decree that all people in my kingdom must be counted. Each of you must return to your ancestral home in Bethlehem. The journey will be long, but follow the star"—he paused, turning to point at the star that hung above the parking lot—"and you will reach your destination."

A little bit of a revisionist version of the Christmas story, but the eager throng of families—mine included—didn't seem to care. Pastor Cal flung open the gate behind him and let the families in one at a time. When it was our turn, Izzy and J.W. tugged us forward.

We entered the maze, which was marked out by bales of straw that were stacked about five feet tall—low enough that adults could see over them to navigate, but the kids couldn't. It wasn't a true maze; there were no dead ends. It was more of a labyrinth, designed to take us on a journey through the Christmas story and act as a petting zoo at the same time.

Every so often, the path through the straw bales widened, and a scene with live actors told part of the tale: Mary and Joseph traveling to Bethlehem on a donkey, for example. The three Wise Men making a longer journey to meet the Christ child with their camels. The shepherds marveling at the star that shone so bright in the sky as they watched their sheep. At each stop, the kids got to pet the animals.

I hung back to watch Izzy and J.W. enjoy the journey, exploring the maze and squealing when a new cute animal appeared around a bend. They even got to feed the camels a carrot, because Rusty was playing one of the Wise Men. By the time we got to the last stop, featuring real cows and a fake baby Jesus in the manger, they were exhausted.

"You said there would be doughnuts," J.W. complained.

"Let me just get a picture to show your dad, and we can go inside." Andrea tugged him over to stand next to Izzy in front of the final Nativity scene. She captured a few shots of them with her phone and then we all headed for the exit—or rather the entrance to the church basement, which was the only way out, a clever fundraising move.

Inside the basement, the crowd hummed pleasantly as folks bought refreshments from the Chamber of Commerce table and stopped by a collection box to drop in a donation to the church, too. Ruth spotted us at the end of the line and left her post to smuggle us a few doughnuts.

"But we didn't pay yet," Izzy protested, when Ruth handed one to her.

"Special treatment for special souls," she said to Izzy. "Your nana can pay me later. Can you spare a minute, Leona?"

I left Andrea and the kids to eat their treats and followed her to a quiet corner of the church's kitchen. "What's up? Do you need a hand serving refreshments?"

"No, it's not that." Ruth gnawed her thumbnail and then sighed heavily. "I think Rusty might be in trouble. Eli came to talk to him this afternoon. *Twice*."

My stomach dropped. One interview was standard. Two interviews meant Eli didn't think Rusty was being truthful. "What happened? Did he change his story or something?"

Ruth shook her head. "He said the exact same thing he told us on the phone."

"So what's the problem?"

"She is." Ruth's eyes went to someone behind me. I turned and saw Joan walking toward the drinks table, where one of the church volunteers was serving some of my apple cider from a steaming crock pot. "Eli interviewed her, too, and she said that when she stopped to pick up the donated toys from the gas station, Homer didn't answer the door. So Eli thinks—"

"That Rusty killed him?" I scoffed.

"Well, is there any other explanation?" Ruth shrugged helplessly. "He was alive when Rusty walked in and he wasn't alive the next time someone saw him."

"Did Joan actually *see* Homer? Or did she just knock and then leave?"

Ruth shrugged again. "I don't think she saw him. If she did and he was dead, she would have called an ambulance, right? And she wouldn't wait around for him to show up and play Santa. She would have let me know that he wasn't coming."

"Unless she thought he was just passed out or something," I said thoughtfully. "Let's go ask her what—"

"Ruth! We need more change!" one of the Knitwits called from the cash box table.

Ruth grimaced at me. "I gotta run."

"Go, go," I urged. "I'll talk to Joan. I bet we can clear this all up."

Ruth darted upstairs to get more change from the safe in

Pastor Cal's office, and I made a beeline for Joan where she was nibbling a doughnut and sipping spiced cider, admiring the ornaments on one of the church's many Christmas trees. When I drew up beside her, she turned to me, gesturing with her doughnut at the yarn angel that hung at eye level, sending a shower of cinnamon-sugar over the branches beneath it. "I made that one."

"It's very cute," I said politely.

"I'm teaching a workshop next fall if you want to learn how to make them." She looked at me expectantly. When I didn't jump at the chance to sign up for a craft class being held ten full months in the future, she turned her attention back to the tree.

"Can I ask—" I began.

"Crochet," she said around her mouthful of doughnut. "It looks like knitting, but it's crochet."

"Actually, what I wanted to know was—"

"Twenty-five dollars. It's a three-hour class, so it's an excellent value." She licked the sugar off her fingers and blew on the surface of her hot cider before taking a sip.

I grit my teeth. "I don't want to make any angels. I wanted to ask—"

"We'll also cover stars and snowmen if you prefer secular designs." She tapped her chest, where a large star crocheted in glittery silver yarn acted as a brooch on her peacock-blue dress.

"Fine. Sign me up." It was worth twenty-five bucks just to get her off the topic. She gave a satisfied nod, and I went on. "Let's talk about when you picked up those donations from Wilds Gas and Go before the first Honeytree Holidays event."

Joan froze, her mouth on the rim of her cider. She lowered

the cup. "I didn't pick up any donations there. I knocked, but there was no answer. I already told the sheriff all of this."

"What'd you do when Homer didn't come to the door?" I asked.

"I waited about five minutes. When he didn't answer, I assumed he was already at the community center, so I left. I didn't want to be late and disappoint the kids."

"You didn't look inside? You didn't see him through the window or anything?"

She shook her head. "Didn't see hide nor hair. Of course, I wish I had, now that we know he'd already passed on."

"Or maybe he was just uninterested in talking to you?" Who could blame the guy, really—Joan was pretty insufferable, judging by the few conversations I'd had with her.

Joan flushed slightly, her hand holding her cider cup trembling. "I suppose so," she said tightly. I guess I could have done a better job wording that suggestion. Oh, well. Maybe it'd get me out of that workshop I didn't want to attend anyway.

"Great, thanks!" I said, already scanning the basement for Eli. Just because Joan hadn't seen Homer alive didn't mean he wasn't alive. It just meant that he didn't answer the door. There was absolutely no proof that Rusty had done anything to Homer.

I didn't see Eli in the refreshments area, so I stopped by where Andrea was supervising the kids while they colored pictures at a craft table. The Sunday school teachers had set it up to keep the kids busy so their parents could actually visit and stocked it with photocopied coloring sheets in a confusing mix of Care Bears and Bible stories.

"I'm going to go find Eli for a minute," I said to her. "Sorry to run out on you again; I'll be right back. If I'm not back here in ten minutes, coloring a picture of Funshine Bear turning water into wine, send me a mean text message." Andrea giggled and nodded, and I headed up the stairs.

Chapter 19

The sanctuary upstairs was empty, save for the echoes of a few people who, like me, were on their way out of the church into the crisp, cold night. When I walked out onto the front steps, it took a moment for my eyes to adjust. The streetlamps in front of the building had been turned off, probably to throw the star above the Nativity into higher relief.

A few snowflakes tumbled lazily out of the sky, like an afterthought. Perfect timing; maybe the kids would wake up to a white Christmas tomorrow. A smile on my lips, I glanced toward the parking lot and spied Eli near the arched entrance, chatting with Pastor Cal. The throng of people entering the maze had dwindled to a mere few, which made sense; the basement was so packed, everyone must have already been through it at least once.

I walked over and joined them, rubbing my hands together to warm them up. No wonder it was snowing; the temperature felt like it'd dropped five degrees since we'd gone through the maze.

"Aren't you freezing your toga off?" I asked Pastor Cal.

"Nope, I've got a pair of genuine Roman long johns on underneath the sheet," Cal said, grinning as he adjusted his golden crown of leaves.

Eli chuckled. "You can warm me up, if you're volunteering." I let him pull me into his side and stuck my hand in the pocket of his jacket, shivering. He rubbed my shoulder, frowning. "We should get you back inside. See you later, Cal?"

Pastor Cal nodded and Eli led me back toward the front doors of the church. But before we got inside, I paused. I wanted to have this conversation somewhere quiet. "Wait. I have another favor to ask you. I know you have to do the whole criminal investigation thing the right way, and you already stretched it by letting Peterson have an extra day, but please, hear me out. I'm sorry I asked you to break the rules for me. And I'm sorry if it seems like I'm meddling in your case yet again."

Eli paused. "It's fine, Leona. You don't need to apologize. I know you're not trying to screw anything up."

"Really?" I looked up at him. The glow from the star cast deep shadows over his face, setting his ridiculous bone structure and long eyelashes into relief. Could I really be so lucky that this man not only loved me, but was quick to forgive my sins?

"Truly." He dropped a kiss on my forehead, and I could feel the resulting tingle spread over my entire scalp. "Now, what do you need?"

"Tell me you're not going to arrest Rusty for Homer's murder," I begged.

The smile faded from Eli's eyes. "I can't promise you that. Right now, he's in a bit of hot water. He admits that he saw Homer alive when he walked into that gas station, but whether or not the man was alive when he left is another matter. All we know for sure is that Homer was dead by the time Joan showed up."

"No, we don't know that! That's what I came to say. He wasn't necessarily dead, he just didn't answer the door. When

139

I talked to Joan—sorry, I had to—she told me that she didn't even see him. Maybe he was just in the bathroom," I added.

"I thought of that. Have a little faith in me, Leona," Eli chided. "Think your theory through to the end. If Rusty didn't kill Homer, who did? Nobody else went inside that building. Rusty is the only one who had motive and opportunity."

I played the security tape in my head, backwards and forwards. Eli was right—the only other person who visited the station that morning besides Rusty and Joan was Ed, and Ed never entered the building. He'd just knocked on the door, filled up his propane tank, and left. Rusty was the only one who went inside.

Poor Ruth. I couldn't imagine how I'd feel if my sibling were capable of something so terrible. It's not that Rusty was an evil person. I'd grown up with him and knew him as a good guy, both hardworking and loyal. But he was also impulsive and emotional, which is why he'd gone to prison to begin with. Now that he was out, he was desperate to find a job and get back on his feet. When Homer canceled the interview, it must have sent Rusty over the edge. He'd grabbed a syringe, filled it with antifreeze, and—

"Wait, where'd Rusty get a needle?" I blurted out. Eli, who'd already started toward the basement stairs, turned back to look at me.

He sighed. "I don't want to believe it, either, but it's not like Homer stuck *himself* in the neck with a hypodermic full of antifreeze. Rusty must have had the needle in his pocket, and who knows where he got it."

"He didn't have pockets—he was wearing elf tights, remember? He didn't have a bag either, not until he came out."

"Maybe Peterson dropped a needle from his med kit when

he was administering first aid," Eli mused. "Rusty could have picked it up. A weapon of opportunity."

I pulled him over to the side, away from the stairs to the basement, to let a family with three kids exit the church. I waited until they were outside the front doors and out of earshot to speak. "I don't think so. That little case in Peterson's med kit was zipped shut, and he had no reason to open it. He still intended it to be my motherclucking Christmas gift at that point. Plus, the case was packed full, right? Another syringe wouldn't have fit in there. The syringe that killed Homer came from somewhere else."

Eli sighed. "What you're saying makes sense, but where does that leave us? All the current evidence points to Rusty, even if we don't know exactly how he pulled it off. And before you say someone hid in the attic and dropped down to kill Homer, then waited until the first responders left before they exited the building, I already checked. I watched Ed's tapes for twenty-four hours before and after Homer's murder and *nada*. It had to be Rusty, even if we never know how he got the syringe."

I gripped his forearm. "That's what I'm trying to tell you, Eli! I know where the syringe came from. It's right there on the security footage. I don't know why I didn't make the connection before."

Eli shook his head, a smile quirking the corner of his mouth. "You know what, Leona? If you were anyone else, I'd write you off as a kooky—"

"Don't say old lady," I warned, holding up my finger.

"I was going to say 'kooky chicken farmer,'" he said bemusedly. "As I was saying, If you were anyone else, I'd write you off, but I'll be darned if you don't have a nose for detective work."

"A beak for detective work," I corrected, ever the kooky

chicken farmer. "Do you want to hear my theory or not?"

"Sure do." He sat down in the nearest pew and patted the hard bench next to him. "I'm primed and ready for your confession."

I ignored where he'd indicated and perched on his knee instead, earning myself a grin so wicked it made my ears burn. I leaned against his shoulder and whispered my version of the crime in his ear. When I was done, his eyes were wide and wondering.

"I think you might have cracked this one, Deputy Davis." His words were joking, but his tone was dead serious. "As reluctant as I am to evict you from my lap, I have an arrest to make."

I hopped up eagerly and followed on his heels as he hurried down the basement stairs.

Chapter 20

As soon as Joan saw Eli and I barreling toward her, she dropped her doughnut—it must have been her second or third—and dashed for the other door. She scrambled up the stairs toward the Nativity exit, pushing her way past the people leaving the maze.

Eli and I followed her as quickly as we could without causing a scene, squeezing through the knots of adults chatting over their hot ciders and weaving carefully between clusters of children as they played on the floor or ran circles around their parents.

At the base of the stairs leading outside, I noticed Joan's doughnut on the floor, the crumbs scattered in an arc behind it. It was the doughnut that had tipped me off. Joan had been so eager to eat it, even licking the sugar off her fingers, but when she stood in front of the North Pole sign at the community center, she'd been downright mean to the Girl Scout who offered her a tiny bit of fudge, snarling that she couldn't have sugar due to her diabetes.

Then, at Knitty Gritty, she'd been gobbling the Knitwits' cookies, and tonight she'd downed doughnuts like they were the cure for her crabbiness. There was only one explanation—Joan controlled her diabetes using insulin injections after she ate. On the day Homer died, she emptied her insulin syringe to deliver a fatal dose of antifreeze. That's why she hadn't eaten any fudge—or any other sweets—at the community center. She didn't have the medication she needed to control her blood sugar because she'd already discarded it. But the following day, when we were wrapping presents for the Gifting Tree, she'd had her insulin available, just like she must have it today.

Moving against the tide of people exiting the Nativity, Eli and I made it to the top of the stairs just in time to see Joan's peacock-blue dress disappear around the next bend in the straw maze.

"Stay behind me," he warned, already breathing heavily as we passed the Virgin Mary. She clutched her baby-doll Jesus to her chest protectively, like it was the real Christ child, as we ran by. "Desperate people are dangerous people."

For once, I listened to him. I couldn't really beat him in a foot race, anyway. His legs were longer than mine and he was in ten times better shape. We passed the shepherds, who hardly seemed to notice the wrong-way chase. The sheep did, though, bleating plaintively. I skidded around the next sharp turn, nearly crashing into the stack of straw.

"We're not going to catch up—she's too far ahead," I panted. Eli was so focused on the chase that he didn't even turn to look at me.

"We have to try," he said. He put his head down and sped up, leaving me in the dust.

My legs flagged, and I slowed to a stop. I literally couldn't run any farther. I started to turn back to the basement when a flash of peacock blue caught my eye on the other side of the wall of straw bales. It had to be Joan, further along in the maze.

I stood on tiptoe to get a better look over the top of the bales.

Sure enough, Joan was heading for the Three Wise Men and their camels. In the other direction, I saw Eli was still two or three turns of the maze behind.

"Rusty!" I hollered at the top of my lungs toward the Wise Men. "Stop her!"

At the sound of my voice, Rusty acted instinctively. He led his camel to the center of the path, blocking it completely. The other Wise Men followed suit. Staring down the huge creatures in her path, Joan slowed to a stop, turning to face Eli as he ran up behind her.

Eli retrieved a pair of handcuffs from the pouch on his belt. "Joan Packett, I'm placing you under arrest for the murder of Homer Wilds."

"You can't prove anything," she spat at him. "You have nothing on me."

"You're on camera, ma'am," he said politely.

She made a disbelieving noise. "That drunk doesn't have cameras."

"But Ed across the street does," I said. I drew on my farm girl upbringing and jammed the toe of my shoe between two of the straw bales, using it to boost myself to the top of the makeshift wall. Straddling it, I said, "You went to collect the Gifting Tree donations from Homer, but something went wrong, didn't it?"

At the sound of my voice, she turned toward me, and her lip curled in disgust when she saw me perched on top of the straw. "Yes, something went wrong. The donations weren't there. So I left."

Eli crept closer to her, and her eyes drifted back toward him. Hoping to keep her distracted, I asked, "What happened to the donated toys?"

"That loser sold them on the internet to fund his little

145

drinking problem," Joan said bitterly. "He stole them out of the arms of children."

I slid down from the top of the straw bales and moved toward her with my hands raised, drawing her attention to me so Eli could inch even closer. "So Homer answered the door when you knocked. He told you he didn't have the toys anymore. And when you realized what had happened to the donations, you were understandably upset."

Color crept up Joan's neck. "I demanded he give me the money he made instead."

"But he refused?"

Joan's eyes flashed. "Oh, he tried. But all he had in the till was a two-dollar bill!"

Rusty's money. He'd been telling the truth. Though I'd believed his story about buying Twinkies with his piggy bank money on its face, I still felt relief flood through my veins. "So then what?"

"He tried to kick me out," she snarled. "No apology, no compensation. Just a 'See you at the North Pole, Mrs. Claus.' And I was supposed to play nicey-wifey to a drunken thief all afternoon?! I couldn't do it. He disgusted me."

I couldn't blame her—I wouldn't have been able to do it, either. But the next step she took? That was unimaginable to me. "So then what happened?"

"He was so drunk he could barely stand, but he popped open a bottle of mouthwash he had on his desk and took a swig. Swished it around and swallowed it. And that's when I had the idea."

Eli was so close now, just a few feet to the side of her.

"What idea?"

"Who would notice one more intoxicant in his bloodstream?

146

I could get rid of him once and for all. No more vulgar language at Little League games. No more fistfights in front of the gas pump. No more drunken Santa stealing Christmas joy from innocent little children." Joan was almost radiant with anger. Above her, the elevated Christmas star cast a bright glow around her, illuminating her even further. "So I pretended to leave and went out to my van. I emptied out the insulin I brought with me so I could enjoy the Honeytree Holidays bake sale treats and refilled the syringe with antifreeze from a jug in his back room. Then I stuck him with it."

Joan jutted out her chin like she was daring me to criticize her choice, her eyes flashing dangerously. So I didn't. "Did he fight back?"

She gave a harsh laugh. "Didn't even notice. He was so sedated, I don't think he felt a thing. It's a shame, really. I would have liked it if he suffered as much as the children who won't get their Christmas gifts will suffer."

One more step and Eli was there. He clasped a handcuff around her wrist, and she let him pull her other arm around into the second cuff, seemingly as unaware as Homer had been when she'd injected him with poison.

"I did the right thing," she insisted, her eyes still trained on me, as though she were looking for my approval.

I couldn't agree with her, although I understood her deep rage at Homer's callousness toward Honeytree's children, the children he claimed to love when he sponsored their sports teams and attended their games.

"I hope you find some peace, Joan." That was all I could muster. She and Eli walked away, following the Nativity maze the wrong way, back out onto the street.

"Phew," Rusty said as he joined me, still leading his camel.

"She's a real piece of work. I thought *I* was ticked off at Homer, but she took it to another level."

I nodded, still stunned by her confession. "Sorry about your two-dollar bill. I'm sure it meant a lot to you, coming from your grandpa."

"Aw, that's all right. I'll figure something out and earn it back. Grandpa always said an honest day's work is worth more than money—it earns you your soul, too. So I'll just keep volunteering around town and eventually it'll lead somewhere. Who knows, maybe I'll end up being a full-time camel wrangler." Rusty grinned at me and rubbed the side of his camel's neck affectionately. The camel leaned its head over to scratch its chin on the points of Rusty's crown.

"Oh my gourd, what's going on?" Ruth asked, jogging toward us in the middle of the maze. She stopped short, slightly out of breath, her wild curls framing her face like a halo in the light of the Christmas star. "I saw you and Eli tear past me like you were being chased by wolves! Rusty's not in trouble, is he?" She pursed her lips at her brother.

"No—he and his camel cop helped catch the real killer," I said quickly, flashing Rusty a grateful smile. "Joan confessed to everything. She killed Homer because he sold all the Gifting Tree donations that people dropped off at the gas station."

Ruth's eyes widened in shock. "Joan? I never would have pegged her for a killer. Well, I'm glad she was caught, but what a blow for the Gifting Tree! Who's going to deliver all the gifts tomorrow? I promised Gary I'd spend the day with him and his girls."

Rusty and I shared a look, and he took one step forward. "I will."

Chapter 21

ndrea turned the rental car into the driveway of Lucky Cluck Farm, where a thin layer of new snow had already blanketed the gravel, softening the hard edges of the stones. The twins murmured quietly in the back seat when the car slowed to make the turn, lulled by the warm cider in their bellies. The multicolored lights on the chicken coop reflected in the snow like jewels, and the gentle glow from the cottage windows melted out into the yard like butter on hot toast.

When I opened the front door, I was met with the scent of something delicious cooking in the kitchen. Herbs and spices mingled into a savory heaven. Peterson had made good on his promise to make dinner for us. Since he'd never lifted a finger in the kitchen as long as I'd known him, I'd tucked away a Plan B in the back of my mind—reheating the ham from yesterday—but I was pleasantly surprised that I might not need to fall back on leftovers.

But before I could get too comfortable, a crash met my ears and I rushed to the kitchen, where Christmas carols were blasting from the radio by the stove. Though the table was nicely set, the rest of the room was completely destroyed. The counters were awash with vegetable peelings, jars of spices, dirty dishes, and empty cans. In the middle of it all stood Peterson, wearing a calico apron with zigzag trim, potholders on both hands, looking horrified. The oven door lay wide open, the handle resting on the kitchen floor.

I grimaced. "I forgot to mention that the hinge is a little fussy. Sometimes it doesn't hold up the door."

Peterson sighed with relief. "Oh, good, I was worried I broke your oven like I broke your—" He didn't finish his sentence, but his eyes darted briefly to the contents of the oven. For the first time, I noticed what was inside. In my big blue roasting pan, a beautifully browned chicken surrounded by carrots and potatoes basked under the heat.

I gasped. "You *didn't*."

Peterson pulled it out and used his foot to close the faulty oven door, and turned to me, his eyes wide. "Oh, no—this isn't your pet! I mean I didn't—I wouldn't—I couldn't—" he fumbled.

I cracked up laughing and let him off the hook. "I know it's not Boots, don't worry. She's a skinny little layer, so she wouldn't make a good roast. Your chicken looks beautiful, Peterson. You did a really great job."

I pushed down the pang I felt at the thought of Boots, still missing. I'd hoped to spend Christmas morning with her on my lap, stealing the raisins off my cinnamon roll while I drank my coffee. But farm life meant sometimes saying unpleasant goodbyes to the animals I loved. I knew that, but the knowledge didn't make it hurt less.

He grabbed his phone from underneath a dishtowel on the counter and checked the recipe he had pulled up on the browser. "Now it says 'rest.' What does that mean?"

I pulled a sheet of foil from the pantry and returned, handing it to him. "It means what it says. Tuck it in like a child at bedtime and let it have a few minutes to get cozy." I called to Andrea and the twins in the living room, letting them know it was time to eat. J.W. and Izzy popped right into the kitchen and found their seats, but Andrea didn't make her appearance.

"Where's your mom?" I asked them as they settled in at the table, spreading their napkins across their laps. Before they could answer, I heard a screech, a clatter, and the sound of the bathroom door slamming shut. A second later, Andrea appeared, her hair slightly mussed, straightening her clothes.

"You try to have a minute to yourself, but no," she muttered under her breath. Lifting her eyes to meet mine, she added, "I think I found your chicken, Mom."

Hope suffused my body. Fingers tingling, I ran through the house to the bathroom. The lid was askew on the hamper, the one I hadn't had the heart to check after the first few days without eggs. I held my breath and peeked under the lid. Under the top layer of clothes, I spied a telltale ruddy feather poking out.

I gently lifted the fabric and was met with a beady, accusing stare. Boots puffed up into a ball, letting me know that she was *not* interested in my attention.

Motherclucker. That's why she'd attacked Peterson. It wasn't some kind of pet chicken intuition. She didn't sense an unwelcome guest. No, the girl was full-on broody, protecting her clutch. I ignored her protests and stuck a hand underneath her, counting six eggs by feel. Who knew how long she'd been setting on them—a week, at least. Maybe longer, I reflected, given how busy I'd been lately, preparing for Andrea's visit.

I dodged Boots's beak and stole one of the eggs, using my phone's flashlight to candle it for development. I had no idea if her eggs were even fertilized, given that her contact with the flock was sporadic. But even in the relatively weak beam of light, it was obvious the egg held a chick. I tucked it back underneath her, chuckling to myself, and left the lid open on the hamper in case she wanted a break to eat and drink.

"Is that the one you were looking for?" Andrea asked.

"That's her—she's setting on eggs. I never would have guessed it; her breed doesn't usually go broody."

"She's having babies?!" Izzy asked. "Can we see?"

"They're just eggs for now," I said. "And she's very protective, but if you want to peek at them, I can show you."

While Peterson and Andrea got dinner on the table, I took the twins to the bathroom. I held Boots, clamping her wings to her sides and turning her so she couldn't derail their investigation of her nest, enabling them to see the eggs she had hidden underneath her.

J.W. felt the surface of the eggs with a gentle finger. "They're hot!" he said, delight spreading across his face.

I nodded. "She keeps them warm until they're ready to hatch, and she almost never leaves the nest."

"She doesn't want them to be lonely," Izzy said thoughtfully. "Kids belong with their parents."

J.W. stared solemnly at the eggs. Then, apropos of nothing, he said, "I miss Daddy."

I set Boots gently back in the hamper, tucking my old T-shirt around her as she clucked at the indignity of it all. Then I ruffled J.W.'s silky hair. "He misses you, too, sweetheart. Why don't you run and see if Gamp made a plate for you yet?"

As full as my heart was, I knew something was still missing from our Christmas. In the quiet of the bathroom after the twins left, I messaged Steven. "Our family isn't complete without you here. Any chance you can catch a red-eye? I know a couple of kids who will be really happy to see their dad on Christmas morning."

Immediately, I could see the three dots, indicating that he was typing back. I held my breath, waiting for his response.

"Mom? Dinner's ready," Andrea called from the kitchen. I stood up and started back to the kitchen, my phone still in my hand. A vibration told me that Steven had texted back.

"I don't want to step on Andrea's toes. Things are complicated."

"Don't be dumb. They're simple." I typed as quickly as I could with both thumbs. "You love her, she loves you, and you have two amazing kids together. Get your butt to Oregon already."

Chapter 22

December 25

I t was still dark out when my alarm went off on Christmas morning. I'd set it early because I wanted to get the cinnamon rolls, which had been rising all night, into the oven as early as possible so they'd be ready to eat when everyone else got up. I balanced the oven door carefully as I slid the pan in to bake so it wouldn't crash to the floor and wake up the twins. J.W. and Izzy were often up at this hour, but last night, they'd stayed up late playing Candyland with Gamp, so I took care not to disturb them with noise from the kitchen.

The coffee pot beeped softly, indicating the carafe was full, and I poured myself a steaming cup. I doctored it with milk and sugar and was just about to sit down when Andrea shuffled into the kitchen, wearing one of my flannel robes. Her hair stuck out like dandelion fluff and she squinted at the light from the vintage fixture overhead.

"Morning, Mom," she mumbled, heading for the coffee pot.

"You might want to get dressed first," I said, sipping the hot coffee. It was just the right temperature—hot enough that I could feel it all the way down, but not hot enough to burn my tongue.

"What? Why?" She filled a mug and sat down with it, hunched over to breathe in the steam. A crackle in the driveway signaled a car had pulled up, but Andrea didn't seem to notice. I stood to peek out the window over the sink and saw Steven step out of a mid-size sedan that he'd parked behind Peterson's Rolls. Between my car, Peterson's car, and the two airport rentals, my driveway had officially reached maximum parking capacity.

"Be right back," I said to her and slipped out of the kitchen. I opened the door just as Steven reached the top step, shaking snowflakes out of his dark hair. He looked so much like Izzy and J.W. that it took my breath away.

"Surprise," he said, spreading his arms out. He carried a small overnight bag in one hand and a dozen red roses in the other. I couldn't help it—my Grinchy little heart exploded. I planted a fierce peck on his cheek and then dragged him into the house.

"Merry Christmas! I got you a Steve," I called ahead to Andrea, who rose to her feet when she saw us, her hand fluttering to her mouth in shock. I giggled at her stunned expression and then ducked out of the kitchen, letting them have a minute together. As I left the room, I couldn't help overhearing their first words to each other.

"You came all this way?" Andrea asked breathlessly. "I thought you were going to stay home."

"I missed you too much," he said. "Anyway, my home is wherever you and J.W. and Izzy are."

I missed the rest of their conversation because the twins tore down the stairs in their pajamas, their feet pounding on the risers. I caught them in my arms when they reached the bottom, squeezing them close. "Merry Christmas, you two."

Izzy wriggled free. "It smells like cookies in here. Is that breakfast?"

I let J.W. go, too. "Cinnamon rolls, actually, and they're almost ready. But I have another surprise for you in the kitchen. Go see what it is."

I shooed them off and sat there on the floor, listening to the sounds of the kids squeal in the other room when they saw their dad waiting for them next to the kitchen table. Messy hair, PJs, hot coffee, and the whole family together—though the presents had already been opened and the stockings thoroughly rifled though, the ham already eaten and the tree already lit, this felt more like Christmas than any other moment this week.

I heard the timer go off and pried myself off the floor to take the cinnamon rolls out of the oven, texting Eli on my way to the kitchen. "Merry Christmas. Breakfast is ready."

He and Peterson turned up a little while later with a pitcher of fresh-squeezed orange juice, and I made a big pan of scrambled eggs to balance out the kids' sugar intake. After we all enjoyed breakfast, Eli and Peterson recruited Steve into their fraternity. They clapped him on the back and convinced him to add a shot of whisky to his coffee, which they drank on the porch in their shirtsleeves.

Andrea peeked out the window to see what they were doing and rolled her eyes. "They might as well pound their chests out there."

I grinned at her. "I think it's cute that they all made friends. It's good for them to have someone to talk to."

"He can talk to me." She meant Steve. She chewed her bottom lip pensively as she leaned back against the counter. "If he wanted to, anyway. I'm not sure he does."

"He can and he should—that's something you can work out with your counselor, if you can't figure it out yourselves. But sometimes he just needs to vent, right? Or shoot the breeze with an objective ear to figure out what he's feeling. I was pretty wound up about it earlier this week when Eli was being so nice to your dad. I thought it'd turn into a bash-Leona party, with both of them comparing notes about why I'm impossible to love. But weirdly, I think talking to each other made both of them like me more, not less."

I sipped my coffee, thinking. I hadn't given either of them enough credit. I assumed Peterson hadn't grown since I left him, that his vision of me was still clouded by anger, like mine was of him. And I believed Eli's view of me might be tainted if he learned about all the unkindness I'd dished out when things went wrong in my marriage. But somehow, through each other's eyes, they both saw me more clearly.

I turned to Andrea and smoothed her hair a little bit so she looked less like me and more like herself. "Steve loves you and respects you and wants to make it work just like you do, so the rest is just the details. You're a brilliant woman and he's a kind man. Between the two of you, you can work anything out."

Her eyes brightened over the rim of her mug. When she'd finished off her coffee, she set it down on the counter between us. "So when we come visit in the summer," she began. She broke off, grinning at my stunned expression. "Yes, I said it—I love it here, Mom. It's so good for the kids to let down their hair a little, get a little grubby, breathe some fresh air. I just wish you had a bigger guest room."

My heart swelled. If Andrea loved Oregon in the winter, she'd never leave after a summer visit. Oregon summers are one of the country's best-kept secrets, in my not-so-humble opinion. "Oh, I do have a bigger one—just wait until you see how I converted the loft in the barn. You'll want to move right in."

"If it's good enough for your Porsches, it's good enough for me," she joked.

After a chilly barn tour and a second round of cinnamon rolls and hot coffee, Peterson packed up the trunk of his Rolls Royce and distributed hugs to everyone in the house—Andrea, Steve, and Eli, who I swear teared up a little at the thought of losing his new roommate. Peterson even kneeled in his Brooks Brothers slacks to squeeze Izzy and J.W. close, with a warmth I'd never have guessed.

He left my hug for last. I walked with him out to his car to say my goodbye. This one was so different than our last goodbye, the day I'd moved out of our Beverly Hills mansion for good. This one was full of comfortable humor and understanding, untainted by bitterness.

I traced the scratch in the gold paint near the gas flap. "I guess you'll have to take this in to get touched up when you get back to L.A."

Peterson's mouth bunched in amusement. "I'll probably just get a new one."

"Probably so," I laughed, nodding. That sounded about right. He'd probably get a new eye to replace the one with the fading shiner, if that were something money could buy. It made me feel slightly less guilty for accepting his overgenerous Christmas gift, knowing he'd replace a whole car over one little scratch in the paint. It proved that money meant less to him than happiness—mine or his—which was really the core of what I'd wanted from him when we were married.

On one hand, it hadn't worked out between us. But on the other hand, when I considered our daughter and grandchildren and the holiday we'd just shared, it absolutely had.

Chapter 23

New Year's Eve

"Happy New Year!" Eli raised his glass of homemade eggnog and clinked it against mine, pulling me into the doorway between the living room and the kitchen, where the bunch of mistletoe hung tantalizingly from the doorframe. He took a deep draught from his glass, leaving a wide, creamy mustache on his upper lip, then tried to plant one on my lips.

I giggled and dodged his kiss. "It's not midnight yet!"

"So? This is a warmup. We need to practice. Anyway, it's midnight in other time zones."

As if on cue, a message from Andrea whooshed into my phone, buzzing the back pocket of my jeans. "Happy New Year, Mom and Eli! Love, the Flint Family in Chicago. P.S. Some of us didn't make it until midnight." A photo accompanied her text—Andrea and Steve snuggled up on the sofa, each cradling a sleeping twin. I held the phone out so Eli could admire it, too.

A smile spread across his face as he wiped off his nog mustache. "I have to say, I miss those kids. I haven't had so much fun since I don't know when."

I remembered the way he'd crawled on the floor to play with J.W. and Izzy, taking on every role they dictated and letting them climb all over him. He was so kind and patient with them, even though he'd never raised children of his own. I was happy he had this chance to experience what it was like to watch a generation grow up. "Grandpa looks good on you, Eli."

His dark eyes twinkled mischievously. "No, Grandpa looks good on *you*." He set down our glasses and pulled me into a tight embrace inside the mistletoe zone, and this time I didn't try to get away.

At least, not until I heard a curious sound from the back of the house. A sweet *cluck, cluck, cluck* was my first clue. The second was the soft sound of feathers flapping out of the laundry hamper. I left Eli's arms and ran to the bathroom.

Boots.

She strutted across the tile, her feathers ruffled, and she clucked even more insistently when she noticed me enter the room. A chorus of tiny peeps answered her from inside the hamper.

"They can't get out by themselves, you silly goose," I said. I plucked my T-shirt from the top of the laundry pile inside the basket, revealing six fluffy, yellow, perfect baby chicks amid a pile of empty eggshells.

The chicks peeped loudly as I lifted them from the hamper to the bathmat next to their mama. Boots spread her wings and nudged them insistently beneath her warm feathers, clucking urgently all the while. Only when she had them safe and warm did she settle down on the mat.

She'd pulled it off—she'd incubated her little clutch in the dead of winter, hiding in the hamper, defending against all marauders, and hatched them all herself. It was, in its own way, a little Christmas miracle. It was the perfect end to this year, one that also promised hope for the year to come.

I gleefully showed off Boots's chicks to Eli and then convinced him to sit by the fire and play checkers to pass the time until midnight, even though he always beat me when we had game nights like this. The point wasn't winning, the point was enjoying the time we had together, because as usual, he had to work on the holiday. And speaking of time...

"When does your shift start?" I asked him. All the sheriff's deputies were on highway patrol tonight to keep an eye out for drunk drivers returning home after a little too much holiday revelry. I was proud of him for keeping the community safe even though I'd miss him.

He grumbled in the flickering firelight. "Too soon. I have to leave right after midnight, like Cinderella, so we won't have too much time to celebrate."

"That's OK. I'll still love you even if you bail on the ball." I grinned at him. "I'll track you down tomorrow and shove that glass slipper on your foot, and we can finish our celebration then."

"I'm hoping for a celebration all year, actually." He slid the *Honeytree Heroes* calendar he'd given me for Christmas out from under the tree, where it was still resting on the velvet tree skirt. He handed it to me, flipping to the first month.

There he was in full shirtless glory, a view I'd probably never tire of. "This must have been earlier in the year," I teased. "You're looking pretty tan."

"September," he admitted, pulling up his sleeve and making a face at how light his arm was compared to the photo. He pointed to one of the dates on the calendar—January 17, my birthday. I noticed for the first time that he'd written on it.

Happy Birthday, Leona! Our first date, way back when.

"Remember? I didn't know it was your birthday when I asked you out, and you didn't tell me until we were already at the movies. I felt terrible that I didn't get you a gift."

"You gave me a pack of Doublemint with one piece missing," I said, smiling at the memory.

"The other piece was in my mouth. Fresh breath was part of the present. You're welcome." He winked and flipped to the next page.

The February model was the firefighter with two Dalmatians that I'd seen in thumbnail on the back cover, but Eli had glued a cut-out of his own face over the poor guy's and taped a giant chicken head over one of the dogs' faces. I cracked up.

When I recovered, a quick scan of February's calendar page showed that he'd filled in many of the squares. Some pointed out significant moments in our relationship, both from when we were high school sweethearts and since I moved back to Honeytree. Others were promises of new adventures.

Trip to the coast to watch the whales.

Winery tour.

You, me, and a bathtub full of rose petals. That one was on Valentine's Day, and I had to say, that sounded a whole lot better than putting on a dress and going to a fancy restaurant. He knew me so well.

I made my way through the rest of the year, laughing at his face pasted over every hunky photo, savoring the memories he'd recorded, and noting the activities he had planned.

"I want you to add things to the calendar, too," he said when I'd reached the end. "Anything you want."

"Anything?" Now it was my turn to be mischievous.

He nodded, his expression dead serious, for once. "Anything. Everything. Happy New Year, Leona."

Read More

Want to read more in the Clucks and Clues Cozy Mystery Series? Visit www.hillaryavis.com to see the full list of titles, download free ebooks, sign up for email updates, and more!

About the Author

Hillary Avis lurks and works in beautiful Eugene, Oregon, with her very patient husband and a menagerie of kids, cats, dogs, and chickens. When she's not thinking up amusing ways to murder people, she makes pottery, drinks coffee, and streams *The Great British Bake-Off*, but not all at the same time.

Hillary is the author of cozy mysteries about smart women who uncover truths about themselves, their communities, and of course any unsolved crimes they happen to stumble across. You can read more about her and her work at www.hillaryavis.com.

Made in United States
North Haven, CT
02 June 2023

37284635R00104